Daisy,
Bold & Beautiful

Daisy,
Bold & Beautiful

Ellie Collins

Fresh Ink Group
Guntersville

Daisy, Bold & Beautiful

Fresh Ink Group
An Imprint of:
The Fresh Ink Group, LLC
Box 931
Guntersville, AL 35976
Email: info@FreshInkGroup.com
FreshInkGroup.com

Edition 1.0   2018

Book design by Ann E. Stewart

Cover art by Matt Collins

BISAC Subject Headings:
YAF011000   YOUNG ADULT FICTION / Coming of Age
YAF019010   YOUNG ADULT FICTION / Fantasy / Contemporary
YAF038000   YOUNG ADULT FICTION / Magical Realism

Library of Congress Control Number: 2018937043

ISBN-13: 978-1-947867-15-4 Papercover
ISBN-13: 978-1-947867-16-1 Hardcover
ISBN-13: 978-1-947867-17-8 Ebooks

DAISY

Bold & Beautiful

Chapter I

Thwomp!

"Ugh! Ah! ...Ow!" D.J. rubbed her throbbing head.

"Great. A *perfect* beginning to this *perfect* day."

D.J. sighed with frustration. This was the second time she had fallen out of this bed. It was smaller than her old bed. Just like this room was smaller than her old room and this house was smaller than her old house.

Somehow, *she* had felt smaller since the move, but she couldn't figure out how that could be when the new house and everything in it seemed to be a miniature version of her old home. Dad said she'd get used to all the changes soon, but D.J. wasn't so sure. There was no time to worry about it now, though. It was time to get up and face the day she had been dreading since she first learned they were moving.

Brushing her long, sandy-blonde hair out of her eyes, she took a determined breath and picked herself up off the floor. Rubbing her aching hip, she walked over to her dresser and debated on what to wear. She had set out her favorite blue dress with sunny-yellow tulips, but that was when she was feeling optimistic and outgoing. Now she longed to just blend into the background until the wretched day was done. She grabbed her most comfortable pair of jeans and a mud-brown t-shirt and hopped into a comfy pair of socks as she made her way to the kitchen.

"Morning, sunshine!" Dad greeted her from the kitchen table, where he was eating an English muffin.

"Hey, Dad," D.J. responded with as much enthusiasm as she could muster. She wasn't particularly hungry, but she knew she'd get an earful if she tried to skip breakfast, so she grabbed herself a bagel. Not wanting to take the time to prepare it the way she normally liked her bagels (toasted with cream cheese), she plopped herself down in a chair and ripped a bite off. Not a good plan; it was hard to chew, and it sucked all the moisture out of her mouth. Setting the remainder of the offending food strategically behind the napkin holder, she hoped Dad wouldn't notice if she just left it. She casually walked over to the refrigerator and got herself a glass of orange juice. She remained standing next to the counter, too nerved up to sit back down.

"Excited for the day?" Dad quizzed.

"Ummm...sure?" D.J. tried to sound positive, but before she could stop them, some of her honest feelings broke through. "I don't know." She sighed. "I'm worried that I just won't fit in. How could I? Everything is different here. Besides, middle school is new to all sixth graders, but all these kids have had months to get to know each other now. I'll be the new, weird kid that everyone will point and laugh at."

"Nonsense," Dad assured. "Remember when Hannah Stephenson started at your old school? I know that was in the middle of the year because I had just come in from shoveling snow when you told me about her. Did kids point at her and think she was weird?"

"Of course not; Hannah is awesome!" D.J. was frustrated, not wanting to see the comparison her father was making. This felt like a completely different situation.

"Well, sweetheart, you are awesome, too." He walked over and pulled her into a hug. "And something tells me that the kids here are smart enough that they'll see that right away."

D.J. felt like she was acting like a spoiled, bratty toddler to be so disagreeable about going to her new school. She knew she had to go, but everything in her wanted to just stay right where she was, in the safety and comfort of her dad's strong arms. She didn't want to argue, but she couldn't help but make one last attempt to avoid the inevitable. "But why do I have to go *today*? It's April Fool's Day, Dad! Everyone will look at me like I'm a big joke and whisper about what a fool I am when I don't know where I'm going or what I'm doing. Can't I wait and start tomorrow...or next week?"

Dad's quiet chuckle rumbled against the cheek she rested against his chest. "Nice try, kiddo," he teased. "You *will* be going to school today. I know you're worried and nervous, but I also know how brave and strong you are. I have all the faith that you're going to do fine. Before I know it, I'm sure I'll have to start turning kids away from play dates and sleepovers because the line will be too long."

D.J. rolled her eyes. Her dad's confidence felt good, but she seriously doubted he had any idea what he was talking about. Dad offered a final squeeze of support and turned to put his breakfast plate in the sink on his way to finish getting ready for work. He stopped and turned at the doorway of the kitchen. "Go ahead and finish getting ready, but don't think I missed your little disappearing bagel trick. If you don't want to eat that, fine, but I want you to get *something* for breakfast."

"Fine," D.J. responded on a defeated sigh. "I'll try a little yogurt or something."

"That's my girl!" Dad cheered over his shoulder on the way to his bedroom.

After choking down a small bowl of yogurt, D.J. made her way to the bathroom to brush her teeth and run a comb through her hair. Studying her reflection in the mirror, she realized that she would have no chance at all of making new friends if she didn't find a way to wipe the surly sourpuss look off her face. She knew just who could help her with that. This was a job for Fern.

She quickly made her way back to her room and threw herself heavily into the bean bag chair by her window. "Well, Fern, this is it. It is time for me to face my *DOOM*! I know, I know... Drama queen much? It's just...I just don't know how to do this! I've never been 'the new girl' before. ...But I get why we needed to move here. It's easier for Dad; he doesn't have to drive nearly as far to work here. He's always been there for me, so I suppose the least I can do is try this for him. Okay...I'm gonna do it. Wish me luck. And have a good day...at least that way *one* of us will!"

D.J. flashed a quick smirk at her favorite houseplant as she gathered her backpack, grabbed a sweater, and threw her shoes on. Fern had been there for her for as long as she could remember and had helped her through a lot of tough days—especially when her mom was sick. She always listened patiently and never judged, so D.J. felt completely comfortable being honest with her, which always seemed to lighten the weight on her shoulders.

"Okay, Dad, I'm headed out," D.J. yelled from the front door.

"Hold up! You're not getting away without a last hug goodbye, young lady!" Dad scolded playfully, as he approached her down the hall. "Are you sure you don't want me to walk you to the bus stop?"

"Thanks, Dad, but I think I've got this." D.J. shuddered as she imagined how it would look to have her dad at the bus stop when the bus rolled up. She pictured him doing something utterly embarrassing, like kissing and hugging her goodbye and yelling, "Have a good day, honey!" as the bus pulled away. It was a horrifying scenario.

"Alright," Dad conceded as he pulled her into a side hug and kissed the top of her head. "Smile when you can today and just be yourself. I know you think I don't know what I'm talking about here, but trust me, sweetheart, everything will work out fine. Maybe we can even celebrate your success tonight with a nice dinner out."

"What? We hardly *ever* eat out!"

"Ah, that's a benefit of living in town now, kiddo." He opened the door. "There are lots of restaurants close by. Some of them even deliver, so we could order out if you don't feel like a night on the town."

"Thanks, Dad; that sounds fun! Have a good day and I'll see you this afternoon." D.J. smiled, truly feeling excited for the first time all morning. She took a deep breath and took her first step out the door.

D.J. traversed the short path of stones that led to the sidewalk, then turned to her left as she surveyed her new neighborhood.

She quickly passed the walkway to the house that made the other half of their duplex. Their old house had stood by itself, and the closest neighbor had been about a half mile away, so it seemed strange to D.J. that they were now sharing a house with a whole other family. She didn't mind, really; it was just another new and different thing to get used to.

She continued toward the corner where the bus was due in a few minutes. She liked her street. The low hum of background noise was new to her, like occasional jets passing overhead and cars working their way through busier areas of town. A garbage truck hissed and clanked a few streets away and a dog barked from a few doors down. Familiar sounds helped to make her feel more at home—birds chirping their welcome to the spring weather and a light breeze whispering through the branches of trees lining the street.

The trees were one of her favorite features of her new neighborhood. Two long, magnificent rows of maple trees ran the entire length of her street. They were big enough that their grand canopies might nearly touch in the middle of the road when they reached their full bloom of summer. For now, their leaves were just beginning to peek out after a long winter's rest, showing off their fresh, bright and brilliantly green beauty. She spied what looked like small bird nests in two of the trees. She made a mental note to remember where they were, so she might catch sight of the hatchlings later in the spring when the more mature leaves would better camouflage their locations.

Movement at the end of the street brought her attention back to her destination. Four or five kids were gathering at the bus stop. Adrenaline rushed through her veins, and for a split second she contemplated running back home. She pushed herself forward, though, focusing on putting one foot in front of another, until she was standing near the other kids. She avoided eye contact, feigning interest in anything that would keep her gaze elsewhere—cracks in the sidewalk, daffodils in the flower bed on the corner lot, window boxes on the house closest to the stop, and the scuff on the toe of her right shoe. The bus couldn't get there fast enough; she didn't know how much longer she could elude the eyes of the other students without seeming rude.

Both boys in the group looked older. They were probably seventh or eighth graders. Laughing and roughhousing with one another, they didn't appear to notice D.J. at all. Of the three girls waiting for the bus, two stood together, whispering back and forth. Out of the corner of her eye D.J. caught them skeptically assessing her up and down. When they giggled, she suddenly regretted her wardrobe choice and wished she had tried harder to convince her dad that today wasn't a good day to start school. She wanted to crawl under a rock and hide.

The third girl stood quietly to her side, and finally curiosity had D.J. sneaking a quick peek. She had long shiny black hair and a cute colorful outfit. She was slightly shorter than D.J., which was saying something, because D.J. was far from tall. The girl was lovely, but what made her beautiful was the warm smile she offered when she caught D.J.'s eye.

The bus came to a stop in front of them and everyone began climbing on. D.J. started to make her way toward the back of the bus out of habit. She found it generally warmer than in the front, although she guessed that wouldn't be as important here, where it didn't tend to get so cold in the winter as it did back in her old town. Black-haired girl slid on her seat toward the window, subtly patted the seat next to her, and flashed D.J. another winning smile. D.J. smiled back and sat next to her.

"Hi. I'm May Chan," black-haired girl said. "You must be new to our school?"

"Hi. Yeah. I'm D.J. Daniels. Nice to meet you, and thanks for sharing your seat with me," D.J. returned with a shy half grin.

"Nice to meet you, too! What grade are you in? Where are you from? Where do you live now?"

"Uh...I'm in sixth grade, I'm from North Bend, and we're in the sixth house down on the left side of Grant Street...on the left side of the house? It's a duplex." D.J. wondered if that was how people usually described their address when they shared a house with another family.

"Oh, so you're really close, then; I'm right around the corner on Fir Street! Well, howdy, neighbor!" May laughed.

D.J. couldn't help but smile along with her, and the tension she didn't realize she held in her shoulders started to melt away. "I'm a little nervous, because my old school was a lot smaller than yours," D.J. confessed. "I'm worried I'm going to be lost all day...probably all *week*."

"Nah. My first day was a little confusing, but I got the hang of it pretty fast. You're gonna love Kirkland Heights Middle School; I just know it." May's attention shot to the front of the bus and she excitedly grabbed D.J.'s arm. "Oh! Here's Payton's stop," she announced with a little bounce in the seat. "I can't wait for you to meet her!"

D.J. followed May's line of sight as new kids began filing onto the bus. One tall, thin girl with auburn hair in a sporty bob cut made immediate eye contact with May. D.J. assumed it was Payton and guessing from the way Payton knew right where to find May, D.J. figured this was their usual seat. She wondered, nervously, if she had taken the spot Payton usually did and if that would make Payton mad.

Payton calmly got in the seat in front of them, pulled her backpack off, and turned toward them. "Hey," she greeted, looking at D.J. with a blank expression. "Who are you?"

Once again D.J. found herself longing for a rock to hide under, interpreting Payton's dry tone as irritated or displeased.

May either didn't notice it or didn't care. She dove into introductions with gleeful enthusiasm. "Payton Parker, this is D.J. Daniels, my new neighbor. D.J., this is Payton, one of my best friends! And don't let her scare you away, D.J.; she's a sweetheart who just doesn't always think about how things will sound when she shoots them out of her mouth."

"Hey! What are you talking about? All I did was ask who she was!" Payton protested. "So, you're new, huh?" She directed her attention back to D.J. "Sixth grade?"

D.J. nodded, signaling Payton had guessed correctly.

"Do you know your class schedule yet?" Payton quizzed further.

"No, not yet," D.J. admitted. It was bad enough not knowing where all the classes were; she didn't even know what classes she'd be looking for!

"No worries," Payton comforted her. "We'll get you to the office and get you pointed in the right direction."

D.J. breathed a sigh of relief. She was going into this nightmare of a day with a few allies. That warm feeling was nearly washed away and replaced with a wave of cold panic, however, when she looked out the window to find they were pulling up to the school. Such a monstrosity of a structure intimidated D.J. by itself, but when she imagined the number of people that building housed, she suddenly regretted eating yogurt for breakfast. She worried she might see it traveling in the opposite direction soon.

But May flashed her excited and supportive smile and grabbed her hand as they got up to leave the bus, so D.J. was able to find her calm center again.

Chapter II

It was chaos, pure utter chaos, D.J. decided as they stepped off the bus. She had never seen so many kids all in one place. A dozen or more buses lined up and students were filing off. That was creating a huge mob of chatting, laughing, raucous tweens and teens in front of the school building. Payton led the way, clearing a path through the crowd to the big set of double doors. May followed closely behind Payton and dragged D.J. along by her hand.

Inside the school was significantly quieter than outside, but no less intimidating. The girls led D.J. along a maze of hallways with doorways and rows of lockers that all looked the same. A bit dizzy from it all, she worried she'd never successfully navigate her way to her classes. She breathed through her panic attack just in time to realize they had turned left and were walking through the main office doorway.

"Good mornin', ladies; how can I help y'all today?" greeted a smiling, kind-looking, middle-aged woman behind the desk. D.J. was surprised to hear such a strong southern accent from someone in Washington state. She couldn't remember ever hearing one like that before, other than from the television.

"Morning, Ms. Honeywell," replied Payton. "This is D.J.; she's new and needs her schedule."

"Oh, yes," Ms. Honeywell exclaimed, recognition crossing her face. "D.J., it's so nice to have you with us! I talked with your daddy on the phone this mornin', and we have everything you'll need today right here." She grabbed a few pieces of paper off the corner of her desk. "Okay, let's see. Here's your schedule and I've added a map of the school. Maybe Miss Payton and Miss May here would be so kind as to help you find your way around?" She paused for a moment, turning toward the clock behind her desk. "We have about ten minutes before the first bell, so that should be enough time to get you headed in the right direction. Also, here's your locker number and combination. If you need anything else throughout the day, you just come on back and we'll take good care of ya. Alright?"

"Um...sure. Thanks," D.J. responded, feeling a little uncertain about how successful she'd ever be at finding the office again.

"Come on!" May encouraged excitedly as she spun D.J. toward the door, "Let's see if your locker is near ours!"

As they swept out the doorway and May directed D.J. to the right, Payton grabbed D.J.'s schedule out of her hand. "Hey, May, you have Mr. Miller for Social Studies in second period, right? Looks like D.J. will be in there with you."

"Yay!" May exclaimed, rubbing D.J.'s arm in celebration. "I think you'll like him; he's really nice. What else does she have, Pay?"

"First period she'll have Study Skills with Ms. Peters; that'll be good because I'm pretty sure Lex will be in there with her. She can help her get to Social Studies."

"Who's Lex?" D.J. asked.

"Lexi Silva. She's a good friend of ours; you'll love her," May assured with a smile.

The group came to a stop in front of some lockers. "Well, here we are!" May announced. "You're number 152, and I'm just down the hall a bit at 138. Pay's locker is on the other side of the hall between us, so we're not that far apart! Go ahead and throw your backpack in your locker. I'm gonna grab my books for my first period L.A.; then we can go find Lex."

D.J. wasn't sure what "L.A." meant, but she was thankful her locker opened pretty easily so she didn't have to embarrass herself with requests for help. Payton made quick work of getting what she needed for first period from her own locker and soon joined D.J. to wait for May. She stood shoulder to shoulder with D.J. (actually, shoulder to mid-upper arm, as Payton was significantly taller than D.J.).

Payton held D.J.'s schedule out for D.J. to see as she continued. "Looks like you're on your own for Language Arts in third period; I can't think of anyone who would be in there with you. You should like Mrs. Langdon, though; she's pretty cool. The best news is that we all have first lunch, so we'll be able to meet up again then."

"L.A." must mean Language Arts. D.J. wondered how different it would be from English class in her old school. She wasn't completely clear what Payton meant by "first" lunch, either. More than one lunch? Of all things, she hadn't even thought to worry about what they might call their classes and how many lunches there might be! She tried to shake off her concerns and, instead, focused on attempting to match up the classes on her schedule with the classrooms on her map. But before she had a chance to find much of anything, May was back with them and D.J. was being whisked off toward Ms. Peter's classroom in search of Lexi.

The trek to D.J.'s first period classroom wasn't too difficult; however, it was hard for her to concentrate on their route when so many things along the way grabbed her attention. A long case displayed many trophies of various sizes and shapes.

Signs hung all around, advertising the upcoming Spring Fling. Most distracting, though, many students milled around them in larger and larger numbers as they approached time for the first bell.

Suddenly May squealed and ran ahead, throwing herself in the arms of another girl slightly taller than D.J. but not as tall as Payton. She had long, dark brown hair that hung in what looked like perfect curls, and she wore a relaxed-fitting blue floral dress. Payton calmly walked up to them. "Hey Lex," she greeted in a bored tone.

"Lex, I'm so glad we caught you," May said as she pulled out of her vice-like embrace with her friend. "I want you to meet my new neighbor and our new best bud, D.J.! You have custody of her for first period, and you need to get her safely to Mr. Miller's class for second period. I want you to take good care of her, okay?"

"Hi D.J.; nice to meet you," Lexi smiled warmly. She turned back to May. "Aye-aye, captain; you can count on me," she assured with a mock salute. "Come on, chica." She threw an arm around D.J. and led her into the classroom. "You're in good hands."

D.J. turned back to wave a quick goodbye to May and Payton just before the growing crowd of students swallowed them.

Lexi pulled D.J.'s attention back toward the classroom. "I sit right over here. There's an open seat next to me; you can claim that one for yourself, if you want."

"Okay, thanks." D.J. said, placing her notebook and pencil down.

Lexi then raised her voice. "Morning, Ms. Peters; this is D.J.; today's her first day."

With dark hair in a messy bun, glasses, and business-style skirt and blouse, the young woman walked over to D.J. and smiled. "Nice to have you with us, D.J.! Did you have a study skills class at your old school?"

"Ummm...maybe? We had study *hall*, but not study *skills*. Are they the same?"

"Not really. In this class you'll occasionally get opportunities to work on assignments from your other classes, but this is really a class to help develop your ability to be a successful lifetime learner," Ms. Peters explained. "I'm sure it'll make sense to you as we go along. If you have any questions or problems, please don't hesitate to chat with me about them."

D.J. thanked her and placed her notebook on her desk, hoping her new teacher was right about everything making sense.

Lexi leaned toward her. "Don't worry; this class is easy," she whispered. "Oooo..." she added, pointing to the cover of D.J.'s notebook. "Those roses are beautiful!"

"Thanks," D.J. said with a smile.

"Did you know that there was a time when the Romans decided to only grow roses and they stopped growing food?"

"Uh...huh...no," D.J. admitted. "What... what did they eat, then?"

"Oh, they didn't. It didn't really work out too well for them."

With that, Lexi turned her attention back to the front; Ms. Peters had begun class.

D.J. didn't quite know what to think about Lexi's odd bit of rose trivia. She shook off her confusion and tried to pay attention to the class.

The lesson focused on the effects of eating and sleeping habits on the ability to learn. Is that why Dad always hassled her about eating a good breakfast?

The class flew by, and before D.J. knew it, Lexi had whisked her into the crowded hallway, then pointed her into a classroom. She waved a quick goodbye and headed the opposite direction toward her next class. Just as D.J. stepped into the room, someone squealed behind her. She turned just in time to be bear-hugged by May.

"How was your first class?" she quizzed. "What'd you think of Lex? Ms. Peters is pretty nice, huh?"

D.J. attempted to answer all of May's questions. She thought her new friend could win the award for Fastest Question Asker in the World. But as May introduced D.J. to a tall man named Mr. Miller and explained to him everything she knew about the new kid, D.J. decided May might just be the fastest *talker* in the world, altogether.

Social Studies flew by even faster than Study Skills. D.J. really liked Mr. Miller. He made everything sound really interesting, and he asked the class lots of questions, so they could think of things on their own, instead of just droning on in a never-ending lecture like some teachers. She was a little nervous, because they seemed to have recently started a new lesson on ancient Greek civilization, and she hadn't been working on that back at her old school. Her old Social Studies teacher had been teaching about the Egyptians. D.J. worried about how she was going to learn what her new class had covered about the Greeks before she got there. So far all she really knew was that Greek names were just as difficult to say and remember as the Egyptians'.

May led D.J. on to her Language Arts class with strict instruction to go straight to the cafeteria after class to meet up with May, Lexi, and Payton for lunch. D.J. entered the classroom and stopped at the door.

Only three desks were occupied, but if she just sat at a random empty one someone might accuse her of stealing the seat. She approached the older woman with short gray hair at the big desk in the front of the class. "Ummm...Mrs. Langdon?"

The woman looked up from the paper she was reading, "Yes?" she responded with a smile.

"Hi. I'm um...I'm D.J. Today's my first day here and I think I'm in this class." D.J. held out her schedule for the teacher to see.

"Oh yes. Welcome, dear! Are you coming from somewhere close or have you traveled far to get to us here at Kirkland Heights?"

"Not too far, I guess. We're from North Bend."

"Oh, okay. Well...you're probably looking for a seat. Let's see...this is third period. I think...Hudson?" she called out, directing her attention toward a boy with short, light brown hair, wearing a bulky sweatshirt and athletic shorts, sitting in the middle of the row farthest from the door. "Are there some open seats close to you?"

"Uh, yeah."

"Good. Would you please help D.J. pick a seat?"

D.J. slowly and awkwardly approached Hudson. "Hi," she greeted with an embarrassed half grin and quick, jerky wave. His eyes were a brilliant, bright emerald green. She didn't want to get caught staring at them, so she dropped her eyes to the floor.

"Hi," Hudson greeted back, sounding similarly uncomfortable. "There's this seat here next to me, and there's this one over here behind me."

"Thanks," D.J. said with a more relaxed smile as she chose the seat next to Hudson. That was followed by a few moments of uncomfortable silence, though, so she opened her notebook, planning to doodle until class began. Her pencil fell off her desk, but before she could bend over to retrieve it, Hudson bent down to grab it for her.

"Oh, see, now you're just missing the point," he said in a somewhat stern, accusatory tone as he straightened back up in his seat.

D.J. panicked for a second, wondering how the vibe between them had gone from mildly awkward to possibly hostile, but then Hudson held up her pencil for D.J. to see. He smiled, and with a goofy chuckle he said, "Get it? Cuz the point broke off?"

The point of her pencil had, indeed, snapped. A snicker escaped her as she got the joke, and Hudson smiled even wider, seemingly pleased with himself for making her laugh. His humor reminded D.J. of her dad's. Suddenly the awkwardness was gone, and she was happy to be sitting next to Hudson.

Mrs. Langdon addressed the class with papers in her hand. "Good morning, ladies and gentlemen. I'd like you all to please set your books aside and take out your pencils. We're going to have a little fun with a five-minute pop quiz on the Greek gods we've learned about so far in our Greek mythology unit!"

Moans, groans, gasps, and grumbles could be heard around the classroom as Mrs. Langdon handed papers to the person at the front of each of the four rows of desks.

"Kindly take a copy and pass the rest back, please. Take your time and be sure to read the directions carefully."

D.J. had no idea what to do. Her English teacher at her old school had been teaching about poetry when she left. She had never learned much about Greek mythology. She panicked, wondering if she should ask if she was exempt from taking the quiz. Would the other kids resent her if she got out of taking it when none of them appeared any more prepared than she was? Would Mrs. Langdon think she was lazy or a troublemaker if she asked?

She looked over some of the questions and panicked even further. Not only did the names of the Greek gods not make any sense to her, but the questions themselves appeared to be written in Greek; she didn't understand *any* of it. Furthermore, from the number of lines provided for the essay-style answers, Mrs. Langdon was practically asking for a book to be written for each answer! A few of the other students were openly complaining, saying things like, "But we haven't even *covered* this stuff yet, Mrs. Langdon!"

"Just take your time and follow the directions. You'll do *just* fine."

D.J. broke out in a cold sweat of indecision. Then she took a deep breath, closed her eyes for a moment, and slowly let her breath out. She figured she could at *least* do what her new teacher had instructed before asking for special treatment. As she studied the words in front of her, she began to smile. She wrote her name and the date at the top of the page, scribbled a few more words at the bottom, turned the paper face-down on her desk, and quietly set her pencil down.

"Okay, friends, you should be wrapping it up. One more minute," Mrs. Langdon warned.

D.J. looked around to find about three quarters of the class furiously writing amid sighs and growls of frustration.

One person blurted out, "What?! We *just* started!"

A minute later, Mrs. Langdon made her way around the room, collecting the quizzes. A few grumbled about it "not being fair" and "*whatever.*" Some students pouted and crossed their arms angrily across their chests. Others were silent as they threw their pencils down on their desks.

When she had collected all the quizzes, Mrs. Langdon said, "Okay, well, wasn't that fun! James, did you have fun with that?"

"No!" came the decisive and surly response.

"Oh, well that's unfortunate," Mrs. Langdon responded compassionately. "How about you, Cyrus? Did you enjoy the quiz?"

"Yeah, that was fun," a kid in the back of the room responded with a smile.

"Really? Would you be so kind as to share with us what your favorite part of the quiz was, Cyrus?" Mrs. Langdon prompted further.

"That you didn't have to take it. You just had to write your name, the date, and 'April Fool's Day' at the bottom," Cyrus explained with a laugh.

Exclamations of confusion and disbelief filled the classroom. Mrs. Langdon quieted them all with, "Right you are, Cyrus! That's what it clearly stated in the *directions*. Then you were instructed to turn the paper over on your desk and wait for it to be collected."

After a moment or two of silence, laughter filled the room and students quickly began comparing notes on who had read the directions and who had fallen for the trick. D.J. shared a smile with Hudson, as they both belonged to the "figured it out" group. He held his hand up and she slapped it in a happy high five.

Chapter III

D.J. carefully followed her map from her Language Arts class to the cafeteria. She was proud of herself for only having made one wrong turn along the way. She joined the serving line and looked around for her new friends. She found them at a table in a corner. May waved excitedly at her.

When she made her way to the table, May patted the seat next to her, just like she had on the bus, while simultaneously speaking passionately to Payton and Lexi. "...I know, right? It was so cool! Now we know that we should always have three DPS, two healers, and one tank on attack. And when it's defense we should have two, two, and two. Hey, you guys want to know what I got in my loot boxes?"

"Oh yeah; I got loot boxes, too," Lexi chimed in.

"Yeah, I did, too," agreed Payton in the borderline-bored tone D.J. was coming to know well.

"But *I* got a legendary," May bragged. "It was Mercy's Devil skin!"

"No fair! I've wanted that skin for *so* long!" Lexi whined good-naturedly. A smile quickly spread on her face, though. "Well, know how it's the Lunar Event? I got Tracer's Rose skin!"

D.J. looked around, wondering if she had somehow stumbled into another dimension. The words being spoken around her appeared to be in English, but she couldn't understand a single thing.

"Oooo...that one's super pretty!" gushed May.

"Okay, I got the best skins of all time," stated Payton with conviction. "I got *two* legendaries in one loot box. I got Widow-maker Odile skin *and* Mei's Lunar Event Luna skin!"

It was the most excited statement D.J. had heard Payton make. She wanted to be excited for her new friend but had no idea what she was trying to be excited *for*.

"Uh...no fair!" protested Lexi. "Widow-maker my main!"

"No *way!*" May disputed. "I think you proved to us last night that your main is *so* Genji!"

"I guess you're right," Lexi conceded with a shrug and a smirk, "since we won *all* five games!"

May and Lexi performed a complex high-five/handshake move that included bizarre sound effects, hair whipping, and hands flying around so fast D.J. could barely follow them. She looked from one girl to the next as she bit into her burrito, wondering if she had been mistaken with her alternate-dimension theory. Maybe something nefarious had spiked the chocolate milk the girls were drinking, and they were suffering temporary insanity. ...Or maybe it wasn't even temporary. She made a mental note to avoid the milk, just in case.

"So, D.J.—" Payton attempted to include her in the conversation. "You a gamer? Into Overwatch?"

"Uh...no, I guess not. What's Overwatch?"

"OMG!" May exclaimed. "Only the best FPS *ever!*"

"What's a...what was it? F—P—what?"

"First-person shooter," Payton clarified. "So, you haven't played Overwatch, but you *do* have an Xbox, right?"

"Uh...no," D.J. admitted, getting the distinct feeling that maybe she should be embarrassed by that fact, judging by three sets of disbelieving eyes all staring at her.

"That's okay," May consoled after a moment of apparent stunned silence. "You're really close to my house, so you can always come over to play with me!"

"Oh...okay," D.J. agreed, although she didn't know how excited she really was at the idea of playing video games. She had always preferred outdoor play to screen time. She didn't want to seem disagreeable with her new friends, though, so she kept that thought to herself. "Hey, do any of you have Mr. Steele next period?" she asked, trying to move to a more comfortable subject.

"Nooo..." all three girls said at the same time with grave faces and slow shakes of their heads. D.J. cocked her head, wondering about the dire mood change.

"Sorry," Payton spoke up, answering D.J.'s silent question. "We don't have him for science. He's...well, not to stress you out or worry you—" She leaned in, speaking in a conspiratorial tone, as she looked around as if to see who might hear her "—But we've heard he's a real hard ass."

D.J. noted the slow nods of agreement and frowns of pity from May and Lexi.

"Don't worry." May put her arm around D.J.'s shoulders in support. "Maybe... maybe every single seventh grader we've ever talked to has been wrong about him."

D.J. looked down at her burrito, wondering if she should even attempt another bite, since her stomach was—once again—beginning to revolt.

Taking note of D.J.'s pointed look at her lunch, Lexi asked, "Hey, did you know the word burrito means "little donkey" in Spanish?"

That mental image threw D.J. over the edge. She pushed her lunch tray aside.

* * *

Mr. Steele's class was on the other side of the building, so D.J. had to hurry to have any hope of making it there on time. She finally made it as the bell began to ring. With her head down, she scurried quietly to an open seat at a work table near the back of the room. She sat down, looked up, and stifled a giggle. Her table mate was Hudson from her Language Arts class. He shot her a quick smile as he opened his notebook. D.J. took a deep breath of relief. She might just make it through this class, as long as she had this familiar face next to her.

The man at the front of the room stood tall, had dark hair in a short cut, and wore a nice suit. He looked to be about as old as her dad. He didn't look *so* scary. Then he spoke.

"Okay, mouths closed and notebooks open," he demanded in a no-nonsense, booming voice. "We need to make up some time due to Friday's fire drill. If you'll remember, we were discussing... *Hudson Alexander!*" The final two words thundered across the room.

Hudson's head shot up. Tension radiated from him and panic showed on his face. D.J.'s gaze bounced back and forth between her table mate and the teacher.

"It appears you have a new lab partner. What's your name, young lady?"

Now it was D.J.'s turn to panic. "Uh—D—D.J.," she stammered. "I...I'm new here," she clarified in nearly a whisper. She slumped in her seat as she realized every eye in the classroom was now directed at her.

"Welcome," Mr. Steele said shortly. Then he apparently lost all interest in her as he returned to his lecture. "Okay, if you'll remember we discussed cellular function and were beginning to explore the similarities and differences of various plant cells— how an onion's cells differ from fungal cells, for instance, and why that might be."

D.J. sat a little straighter in her seat. They hadn't been working on cells at her old school, but the mention definitely captured her attention.

"I assume you have all completed the reading over the weekend and understand the material in abject, crystal clarity. Now each lab team will prepare slides containing the cells of two different plant forms, view them, and document your observations in detail. I expect your reports by the end of class."

Some students groaned and sighed, but she had to fight to contain her excitement for the assignment. Hudson showed her where the supplies were kept, and together they prepared the slides for viewing on their microscope.

Caught up in her fascinating discoveries, she was shocked when Mr. Steele announced time to clean up and get the reports turned in. She couldn't believe the whole class had passed by; she had completely lost track of time.

"You just *plant* yourself down in this seat and finish writing up our report. I'll just *slide* over here to clean up our table," Hudson said. He quickly followed it up with the same goofy laugh she had first heard in Language Arts, saying, "Get it? *Plant* yourself? *Slide?* Because these are *slides of plant cells?*"

"Yes. I get it." D.J. rolled her eyes and shook her head, but she couldn't help but laugh.

When she got to Mr. Steele's desk to turn in their report, he tipped his head closer to her and said quietly, "It's nice to have you with us, D.J., and I'm sorry if I caused any embarrassment when I called you out earlier. If you have any questions or concerns about your assignments, feel free to speak to me any time, okay?"

"Okay," D.J. agreed with a smile. She had dreaded this class, but she had so much fun that now she dreaded the wait to get back to it the next day!

*   *   *

By the time D.J. stepped off their bus that afternoon, she was exhausted and ready for some quiet time at home. May had invited her over to partake in a gaming session she and Payton had planned on the bus ride, but D.J. declined, saying her dad would worry, not knowing where she was.

"Hey!" Dad greeted her as she walked through the door. "There's my girl—still all in one piece and everything! How was your first day?"

"Good, I guess. Tiring, but not too bad. I have a lot of homework, though; I feel like I'm starting off behind in a bunch of my classes."

"Wait a minute. So...the world didn't come to an end?" Dad put one hand on his hip and rubbed his chin as if deep in thought."Huh...I thought for sure after all your doomsday, apocalyptic predictions this morning that life as we knew it would *surely* cease to exist," he teased as he pulled her in for a quick hug. "Glad you had a good day, kiddo. Why don't you get yourself a snack and start in on that homework? Then we'll pick a restaurant, head out for dinner, and you can tell me all about it."

Chapter IV

D.J. tumbled into bed at about eight that night. She had done her math, prepped for the science lab planned for the next day and done some Social Studies reading about ancient Greek civilization. She still had some Greek mythology reading to do, although she didn't know how much she'd be able to get done before sleep would take her over.

With her big book of myths resting on her chest, D.J.'s eyes were soon drooping shut, and she fought to open them back up. Then they sprang open when she realized she wasn't in her bed. She was lying on a smooth stone bench in the middle of the most spectacular garden she had ever seen. She sat up with a start and slowly absorbed the majesty that surrounded her. The brilliance brought tears to her eyes.

Just behind her stood a magnificent weeping willow. The grand, sweeping canopy of delicate foliage just reached the bench D.J. sat upon, and offered the perfect blend of filtered sunshine through the sage-colored leaves as they danced upon the gentle breeze. The seemingly never-ending garden was speckled with other trees—mostly what looked to be flowering fruit trees—but what held D.J.'s attention was the sea of intense, vivid color, stunning beauty comprised of every imaginable flower.

D.J. stood from the bench and began to slowly work her way down one of the meandering moss paths. The garden teemed with flowers of every height and type—trailing vines of flowers, exploding bushes of flowers, tall and proud solitary flowers—from the massive, booming blooms of sunflowers to the delicate, petite petals of forget-me-nots. Butterflies fluttered, and bumble bees buzzed from bloom to bloom, reveling in the floral glory. D.J. could explore the garden for weeks and still not discover it all. She stopped for a moment, closed her eyes, and took a deep breath, allowing the breeze to bathe her in the incredible mix of fantastic fragrances.

"Well, hello there!" D.J. startled at the unexpected sound behind her. She turned and sucked in her breath. A young woman approached, her striking beauty rivaling the garden's. Full copper-colored curls that nearly reached her waist were topped with a gorgeous flower crown. Her emerald-colored eyes sparkled, her cheeks glowed with a slight blush, and she wore a friendly, teasing smile on her full, rosy lips. Her long, flowing gown matched the green of her eyes perfectly, and was accented with flowers that almost seemed to bloom from the gown itself. At a loss for words, D.J. simply stared, wondering if such perfection could conceivably be real.

Then the vision of loveliness giggled! "Sorry; I didn't mean to startle you. It's not often I get guests in my garden, and I was excited to meet you," she explained as she stepped a little closer.

"Th...this is *your* garden?" D.J. asked, in an awed, breathless whisper.

"Uh-huh!" she exclaimed excitedly, as she spun around with her arms outstretched, "Isn't it simply *glorious*?"

D.J. couldn't help but share in the exuberant, celebratory mood. "Yes! It's amazing!" she giggled, as she performed a pirouette of her own.

"That's the spirit! Come on!" the gorgeous girl cheered as she waved for D.J. to follow and began skipping down a path with a laugh that tinkled and jingled like wind chimes singing on a slight summer breeze.

D.J. fell into step behind her lovely leader and fought the temptation to stop for closer inspections of unfamiliar flowers. When they rounded a curve, D.J. stopped short at the sight of a tiny gurgling waterfall that seemed to originate from a wall of roses. It fed into a spectacular pond filled with a wide array of gorgeous water plants of every color, from the whites and pinks of lilies to the bright yellows of marsh marigolds. Extraordinary irises and lotus plants of every color stood out, too, along with more unfamiliar blooms that D.J. couldn't wait to learn about.

Her companion spun around to gauge D.J.'s reaction, then laughed and threw herself down onto a soft patch of grass near the water's edge. "I know, right? Isn't this just the best place in the world?"

"I...I don't even have the words for it. It's...breathtaking! Beautiful! How...how did you grow all of this?" D.J. asked as she sat down alongside her new friend.

"Oh, growing is my favorite thing in the *world*, Daisy Jane," she shared on a reverent sigh. "There is no better feeling than when you're nurturing life. How could you not rejoice at the birth of a little shoot of green perfection as she peeks above the soil's warm, protective embrace for the first time, so she might gaze upon the majesty of the sun? How could you not dance with joy when she reaches up with all her might, opens her arms, and bursts forth her beauty, sharing it so unselfishly with the rest of the world?" As she spoke, she gently caressed the bud of a young flower. Before D.J.'s widening eyes, a perfect blush-colored bloom unfurled.

"That's...that's amazing," D.J. whispered. Then she gave her head a bit of a shake and her brows came together as she thought about what, exactly, had just been said. "Wait a minute. How did you know my name is Daisy Jane?"

"Oh, I was so excited to find a new friend, I'm afraid I completely forgot my manners! Hello," she formally greeted with a friendly smile, "I'm Persephone, and it's a pleasure to meet you!"

"It's very nice to meet you, too, Persephone; but how did you know my name? Most people just call me D.J."

"Oh, I think your mom was simply *brilliant* when she decided to name you Daisy Jane. It's absolutely perfect, don't you think?"

"I don't know. I always worry that people will think my name is hokey if they know what D.J. stands for. I mean...who names their kid *Daisy* anymore? Wait—you knew my mom?"

"Nonsense," Persephone admonished. "Daisies are the embodiment of purity, innocence, beauty, patience, new beginnings, and true love. Why *wouldn't* mothers gift their daughters with such a delightful name? And yes, Jane was an amazing woman." She paused and looked at D.J. with a perfect countenance of genuine sorrow and grief. "And I'm so incredibly sorry you had to say goodbye to her so soon."

D.J. hated the uncomfortable, conflicting feelings that rose within her at the mention of her mom's passing. She fought to tamp down the tears that wanted to leak from her eyes. In the end, curiosity ruled out, though. "How did you know her?" she asked quietly.

"Oh, she helped me, of course!" Persephone's smile was back in full force. "As you know, she could convince even the most temperamental plants to grow and thrive. Her greenhouses and the many, many marvelous plants she raised over the years helped to spread the joy of gardening around the world!"

D.J. beamed with pride. She found it refreshing to be reminded of what her mom was best at rather than dwelling on her illness and passing. "You're right," she agreed. "Mom was a great gardener."

Persephone reached over and pulled D.J. into an embrace. "And you are, too. You'll always have that part of your mom to carry on with you and to gift the rest of the world with."

D.J. relaxed as warm, soothing and peaceful feelings of hope and joy washed over her. "Come on," Persephone encouraged her as she jumped to her feet. "Let's go explore some more!"

With that they were back to skipping along the paths, laughing and clapping, oohing and ahhing, as they encountered exciting new blooms. Before long, though, Persephone stopped, cocked her head to the side for a moment, and said, "Oh, bummer. It's time for you to go home. You don't want to be late for school."

"School?" D.J. asked, confused.

"Yeah," Persephone answered with a disappointed sigh. "You'll come back later, but for right now, Daisy?"

"Yeah?"

"Don't roll to your left."

"What? What do you—"

Thwomp!

"Ugh! Ah! ...Ow!" D.J. reached up to rub her head as she opened her eyes and sat up...on her bedroom floor. She burst out laughing. Looking up at Fern, she gushed, "OMG, girlfriend, you would have *loved* the garden I just visited! It was *insane* it was so cool! And..." She stopped and frowned a bit. "And it was just a dream, I guess. Huh...it...it felt so *real!* But...here I am, sounding like a crazy person telling you about the greatest garden ever." She sighed. "Well...it was still really cool, and I'll tell you about it when I get home. Right now, I guess I'd better get ready for school."

D.J. picked up the book of mythology that had fallen off the bed, then made her way over to her dresser, where she felt inspired to wear something that popped with bright, vibrant colors.

* * *

D.J. made her way to her classes with a little more confidence than the day before. She didn't think she would be feeling nearly as self-assured without the presence and support of her new friends. From the moment she arrived at the bus stop that morning and May pummeled her with a suffocating hug, she felt accepted and supported.

She began to feel somewhat left out at lunch, though, when the girls broke into another deep discussion about the video games they had played the night before. She used the time to reflect upon her own night's excitement. She still couldn't believe her time with Persephone had just been a dream. She couldn't recall ever having a dream including smells. She couldn't figure out how she could have had a dream about plants and flowers she'd never seen before, either. Her imagination wasn't big enough to conjure up even half of what she had seen.

Dream or not, D.J. was inspired to do some planting. She and her mom had a tradition of starting the planting season on her mom's birthday, April 25th, but she thought she might get an early start this year. She'd still plant some more on the 25th to honor the tradition, but she just couldn't wait to get started. She wondered if her dad would mind taking her to the garden store after school. She'd start with some pansies...and maybe daisies. She smiled at the memory of what Persephone had said about the flower she had been named after.

"...Yo! Earth to D.J.!" Payton's words broke through D.J.'s reverie. Shaking her head a bit, she looked from one girl to the next with raised eyebrows, silently asking, *Huh?*

"What's up with you, Deej? We asked you a question, like, three times," scolded Lexi.

"Sorry. I was just thinking about...about a dream I had last night." D.J. nearly cringed at how lame she thought she must sound.

"Hey, did you know that people somewhere in China used to sleep on their loved ones' *graves* so they'd be visited by them in their dreams?" Lexi quizzed in a hushed voice, as if she were telling a ghost story.

May rolled her eyes. "Enough with your weird history trivia, Lex; this is about D.J." May turned her attention back to her new friend. "I was just asking if you asked your dad about coming over this afternoon to game with us," she explained.

"Oh." D.J. scrambled to respond in a way that wouldn't alienate her new friends. "I didn't know you'd be playing today, so...I kinda made other plans." At least she hoped her dad would agree to take her to the garden store so it would be a plan and not just a wish.

"Didn't know we'd be playing? What do you mean? What *else* would we be doing?" Payton scoffed.

"Oh yeah; I guess you're right." D.J. laughed nervously. "Maybe another day?"

"Alright. I suppose you're excused for today, but you *will* be walking your butt to my house with me tomorrow, young lady!"

D.J. laughed. "Okay!" Then she wanted to change the subject, fearing the girls would ask her about her all-important plans. She didn't really think they'd laugh at her if she told them, but she was afraid they wouldn't understand. "So, what's the Spring Fling all about? I've been seeing posters all over the place. It's next Friday, right?"

"Oh yeah; the Spring Fling is *awesome!*" explained May. Lexi nodded her head in enthusiastic agreement. May continued, "They have all these booths and games that raise money for the PTA; then the whole night ends with a Sadie Hawkins dance."

"Did you know Sadie Hawkins was a comic strip character?" Lexi threw in.

"I was thinking about asking Jake Howard," May announced, ignoring Lexi's fun fact. "Pay, you should ask Mike Tomkins; you two would look cute together!" she continued with a mischievous sparkle in her eye.

"Yeah," Payton said in a tone that dripped with sarcasm, "I'm all about 'cute'. And I just go *weak in the knees* at the thought of dancing with Mike Tomkins." She rolled her eyes.

"Oh, you know you want to! You guys would be *adorable* together!" May was unfazed by Payton's response. "Lex; how about you? Who are you going to ask?"

"Hmmm...I don't know. What do you think of Marco Lopez?"

"OMG. He's a total hottie. You go for it, girlfriend!" May exclaimed. She jumped up and initiated one of their intricate high-five/handshake moves. This one included a chest bump, a 360-degree spin, and a dab. D.J. was amazed. She wondered how they came up with these crazy things, deciding YouTube must have an instructional video or something.

"Alright, Deej...we've gotta come up with someone for you to ask." May turned to her in all seriousness.

"How about Sawyer Patterson?" Payton threw in.

"Mmm...I don't think so," May decided after tossing her head back and forth in thought for a few seconds. "If he even agreed to go at all, he'd be in the bathroom the whole time, staring at himself in the mirror. *Way* too in love with himself."

"What about Bode McKenzie?" Lexi suggested.

"Uh, *no*," May said decisively with a shake of her head. "Too picks-his-nose-and-eats-it."

"May. That was in *first* grade," Lexi argued. "Are you ever going to let him live that down?"

"Uh, *no*."

"What do you guys think about Hudson Alexander?" D.J. asked in a small voice that she hoped nobody else would hear. She hoped even more that the girls wouldn't laugh at her or pick on her for her choice.

"Hudson Alexander?" Payton asked with a skeptical raise of her brow. "Pfff... If you can get him off the soccer field long enough to do anything other than change into a new pair of soccer shorts...sure, go for it! Be sure to have a soccer ball in your hands when you ask him, though; it's probably the only way you'd get his attention."

"I don't know that I've ever heard the boy speak," Lexi threw in. "—Well...other than when he's showing off in gym class and announcing his own moves. 'He shoots! He *scores!*'" she mocked.

"OMG, he's like...a male Tracer!" observed May.

Payton laughed. D.J. didn't recall ever having seen her laugh before. Apparently, it was a rare occurrence. May and Lexi both shot her looks filled with as much surprise as D.J. felt.

"Sorry," Payton apologized when the shock of her audience registered. "I was just picturing him dressed up as Tracer, running around the soccer field."

May and Lexi laughed along. D.J. was confused.

"Oh...we'd better lay off the Overwatch references; D.J.'s eyes are glazing back over," Payton warned.

May cleared her throat. "Sorry. But... Hudson *is* quite the jock."

"Really? He's in a few of my classes," D.J. admitted, "and...I don't know...he seems...nice. He makes me laugh."

"Huh," all three girls said in harmony with matching looks of "whatever you say".

"Well, I guess he's not a *bad* guy, so... sure!" May encouraged out loud. "Give it a shot; see what he says!"

D.J. didn't know about *actually* asking Hudson to the dance. She had never asked anyone to a dance before. She didn't know if she'd be able to gather the courage in time for Spring Fling.

Chapter V

After school, D.J.'s dad happily drove her to the garden supply store to pick up some necessities for planting. At home she set up a potting station near the window in her room and eagerly began her project. She settled into the calm, relaxed, familiar task of potting, relishing the feel of the rich, dark soil running through her fingers. She regaled Fern and her new pansy and daisy seeds with tales of Persephone's garden as she lovingly put her fresh, new babies to bed in their pots. When she was done, she beamed with pride. She couldn't wait to see how beautiful her new flowers would be, and she looked forward to the excitement of transplanting them outside when the time was right.

D.J. was unusually excited for bedtime that night, hoping to be gifted with a return trip to the garden. She got herself situated, propped up on her pillows with her book of Greek myths in hand. Mrs. Langdon had mentioned a Persephone in her Language Arts class that morning, so D.J. looked Persephone up, wondering if it was *her* Persephone.

The goddess described in the book was the daughter of Zeus, King of the Gods and Demeter, the Harvest Goddess. Persephone's title was Goddess of Spring. That made sense to D.J., since her mom was the Harvest Goddess, but Persephone was also called the Queen of the Underworld. D.J. couldn't understand that part; she wondered what possible connection a Goddess of Spring would have with the Underworld.

"Trust me; it's a long story." D.J. was startled from her musings by Persephone, who was suddenly sitting next to her. They weren't in D.J.'s bed, though; they were back in the garden, resting against a wall of delicious-smelling Honeysuckle.

"So, they're talking about *you* in the book, then?" D.J. asked.

"That's me!" Persephone confirmed with a smile.

"Well, now I guess I can see why your garden is so spectacular...with you being the Goddess of Spring and all. But...what's with being the Queen of the Underworld?"

"Ugh," Persephone grunted. "*That* title I got through marriage."

"You're *married*?" D.J. was shocked. Persephone looked like she was either a senior in high school or had maybe just started college.

"Yeah," Persephone confirmed on a long-suffered sigh. "I don't want to think about that right now, though. Come on. Let's go do some pruning." She jumped up and started down one of the moss paths. "So, how was your day?"

D.J. followed her. "Oh, fine, I guess. There's something called a Spring Fling coming up."

"That sounds fun!"

"Yeah," D.J. agreed. After a moment's hesitation she continued. "But...I'm a little nervous about it. Girls ask the guys to go to the dance. There's a guy I'm thinking of asking, but I just don't see myself having the guts to actually ask him."

"Oh! What's his name? I bet he's cute, isn't he?" Persephone teased.

"His name is Hudson, and yeah, he's cute," D.J. admitted with a blush, "but what I like most about him is that he's really funny."

"That sounds like Hermes," Persephone revealed as she walked up to a rose bush. A few pairs of trimming sheers sat nearby. She took one set and handed the other to D.J. "He was a real trickster," she continued as they began to snip away at the overgrown sections of the bush. "He was nice, he was cute, and he flirted with me a little bit, but what I like the most is how much he made me laugh."

"Did you ever go to a dance with Hermes? Or date him?" D.J. asked.

"No." Persephone laughed. "My mom was uber-protective. It drove me nuts. Hermes and another guy, Apollo, asked her if they could go on dates with me, but she would have *None. Of. It!* I would just see Hermes from time to time at the big gatherings, like the Olympic games. He was really easy to talk to and he goofed around a lot. It was fun." She smiled.

"Is...is that who you married?"

"Ha! I wish! No. There was another guy—Hades. I didn't know it at the time, but he had decided he was in love with me. He heard that Mom wasn't allowing anyone to date me, so he went to my dad." They moved on to trim another bush.

"Zeus?" D.J. asked.

"Yep. And I don't know if Dad was distracted with some world crisis or something, or if he just didn't care, but he told Hades, 'Sure, no problem! Of course you can date my daughter!' Not that he thought to ask *me* first, mind you. I never would have agreed to date Hades! He's so...*goth*...always dressed in black, broody, no sense of humor...just a real downer. Know what I mean?"

D.J. nodded.

Persephone continued, now with a raised voice in something of a rant. "And then he couldn't just come around offering me gifts and taking me out on dates like a normal guy would do. Oh no. He had to be all *dramatic* about it and over the top. I was out just playing in a flower field with some of my nymph friends one day, and out of nowhere here comes Hades in his *black* outfit, riding in his *black* chariot, being pulled by his big *black* horses, and he just scoops me up and carries me away to the Underworld before I even know what was going on!"

"Seriously? So, he just...like...*kidnapped* you?" D.J. was horrified.

"Yep. He didn't hurt me or anything. After all, he worships the ground I walk on," she said with no hint of arrogance. "Still, though; how *rude!*"

"Well..." D.J. could hardly imagine such a situation. "What did your mom say? I mean; you said she was really protective, right?"

"Oh, she *Blew. A. Gasket.* Like...*totally* lost it," Persephone explained with a shake of her head. "She refused to tend to her harvests, and that led to widespread famine. Dad got so sick of complaints about people starving that he ordered Hades to let me go so Mom would go back to growing food."

"Wow," D.J. breathed. "That's intense!"

"I know, right? Talk about your family drama!"

"Makes me thankful for my dad. I mean, sure, he's a total dork sometimes, but he really gets me. And he's always there for me."

"Uh, that puts him in the category of Best Dad *Ever* in my book!" praised Persephone. She glanced about, taking in the spectacular garden. "Hey, I know of a bit of bare ground that is just begging for some new seeds!"

With that they explored the maze of moss paths—laughing, skipping, and stopping occasionally to smell and pick beautiful blooms.

* * *

"Dad, is it okay if I go over to May's house for a few hours after school today?" D.J. asked over her bowl of cereal the next morning.

"Sure. She's the one who lives just around the corner, right?"

"Yep."

"What do you girls have planned?" Dad quizzed.

"Mainly video games, I guess."

"Huh. I didn't know you were into video games; you've always seemed more interested in outdoor activities...like the gardening you couldn't wait to get started on yesterday."

"Yeah," D.J. admitted, "I can't say I'm psyched about playing video games, but...I really like the girls; they're *super* nice, so I don't mind doing it if it means I'll get to hang out with them."

"That makes sense, I guess." Dad nodded. "However, just remember that friendship goes both ways. Right? If they want to share their gaming with you, that's fine. But that doesn't mean that you have to just play games with them to remain friends. If they truly want to be friends, then they'll be open to experiencing things *you* like to do, too."

"I don't think they'd be into gardening, Dad," D.J. was sad to have to admit. "Plus, there's three of them. Maybe one of them would be willing to do stuff that I like to do, but I don't know about all three, and they're all so close that they're going to keep doing what they all like to do. Know what I mean?"

"I see your point, but if all three girls are *truly* your friends, then all three would at least be willing to try an activity that you like...just like *you're* trying something they like." Dad paused for a moment, then added, "In the meantime, why don't you check out what types of groups and clubs there are at school? There's lots of them—chess clubs, drama clubs...maybe there's a gardening club. If these girls try gardening and don't like it, you could still hang out with them from time to time, but if you found a gardening club to get involved in, you'd *also* be able to hang out with kids who have more in common with you, doing stuff you truly enjoy."

"I guess I could ask," D.J. admitted. By that, she meant she could ask about what groups and clubs were at the school. She couldn't see herself asking May, Payton, and Lexi to do gardening with her. What if they said no? What if they laughed at her for having such an old-fashioned hobby? What if they wouldn't want to be friends with her anymore? She didn't want to think about the possible consequences. It would be easier just to play video games with them. How bad could it be? They obviously had a lot of fun doing it.

* * *

At school, D.J. waved goodbye to May and Payton as they all broke from their lockers and headed to their first class. Before heading to Ms. Peters' study-skills class where she knew Lexi would be waiting for her, she popped into the office.

"Well, hi there, Miss D.J." Ms. Honeywell welcomed her warmly in her smooth, southern accent. "How can I help you this mornin'?"

"Good morning, Ms. Honeywell. I was wondering if you have a list of after-school groups and clubs."

"On the bulletin board right there behind you. Were you lookin' for a club in particular, sweetie?"

"Um, yeah," D.J. admitted, "I was wondering if there happens to be a gardening club?"

"Oh, I don't believe there's a club like that here at the school," Ms. Honeywell said in a regretful tone. "However," she added brightly, "you may want to talk to Mr. Steele. If I remember correctly, I believe he's the leader of a 4-H club that gardens. He was boastin' just this last fall about how the members of his group did really well competin' at the fair with fruits, veggies, and plants they had grown last summer."

"Oh, that sounds awesome," D.J. smiled excitedly. "Thank you very much, Ms. Honeywell; I'll ask him about it this afternoon in science class!"

* * *

D.J. anxiously made her way to science class from lunch, hoping to get there early enough to talk to Mr. Steele before class started. She found a few students in their seats and Mr. Steele preparing for the day's lab. She set her books down at her own seat, said a quick hello to Hudson, and told him she'd be back in a minute, that she just had to ask Mr. Steele a quick question.

"Wait," he stopped her, "you're going to go up there and...talk to him on *purpose?*"

"Yeah," D.J. said with a smile. "What's wrong with that?"

"It's just...he kinda a has a reputation for eating students for breakfast," he explained in a whisper. "*Nobody* disturbs the beast. Word is that the last person who approached his desk without being told to was a poor dude back in 1992. He was never seen alive again..."

"Stop that!" D.J. scolded him with a roll of her eyes. "Mr. Steele is just fine. I just have a question for him. I'll be right back."

Hudson shook his head disapprovingly with a worried look on his face as D.J. approached the front of the classroom.

"Hi, Mr. Steele," D.J. greeted once she was at the teacher's desk. "I was talking with Ms. Honeywell this morning, and she mentioned you might be involved with a 4-H group that focuses on gardening. Is that true?"

"Yes, yes it is," he confirmed. "I began a group a few years back when my kids started getting interested. We meet every Tuesday evening, year-round. We work on various planting and growing projects, from growing vegetables for the local food bank to preparing hanging flower baskets for the Kirkland Heights Nursing Home. We also prepare displays for the Evergreen Fair, which is fun. Last night we were actually discussing plans for this summer's fair display. Why do you ask?"

"Well...I really like to garden, and I was hoping that maybe there'd be room in your group for another person?" D.J. asked hopefully.

"Sure," Mr. Steele responded warmly. "There's always room for fellow gardeners!" He grabbed his briefcase as he spoke, rummaged through it, and handed D.J. a flier that listed the time and location for the meetings. "We'd love to see you there next week, D.J., and great job on Monday's lab, by the way; you made some very thoughtful observations!"

"Thanks," D.J. responded with a half smirk, feeling a little embarrassed by the praise. "I'll tell my dad about the 4-H group, so he can take me next week." She returned to her seat.

"What happened?" Hudson demanded. "I didn't hear any yelling, there were no books thrown, no weapons of mass destruction..."

"Would you stop that?" D.J. tried not to laugh at his ridiculousness. "Mr. Steele is great!"

"Ha! —says the girl who just started here a few days ago! What did you have to ask him, anyway?" He looked around conspiratorially and lowered his voice. "Where he hid the bodies?"

"No!" D.J. couldn't stop giggling as she explained her "visit to the dark side".

"Gardening? Mr. Steele?" he asked. "Huh. I never would have guessed. And you like gardening?"

"Yep, and his group meets every Tuesday, so I'm going to give it a try next week."

"Wow...you're brave!" he complimented with a warm smile.

D.J. laughed, shaking her head and rolling her eyes again. On the inside, though, she was thinking, *"I don't know about that. I'm still not brave enough to ask you to the Spring Fling dance!"*

Chapter VI

"Mom! I'm home!" announced May as she held her front door open for D.J. She threw her backpack onto a nearby bench.

"Hey, sweetie. How was your day?" asked a woman who looked like an older version of May.

"Good. Mom, this is D.J. We're going to head downstairs to the playroom for a little while."

"After you empty the dishwasher, of course," May's mom said with a raised eyebrow.

May huffed. "Mom, I can do that later. D.J. wants to play games, so I wanted to do that first."

May's mother turned her attention to D.J. and smiled. "D.J., it's very nice to meet you. I hope you will excuse May for the *five minutes*," she directed a pointed scowl at her daughter, "it will take her to complete a *single* household chore before she sits herself down in front of a screen. Usually the rule is *all* household chores *and* homework will be completed before screen time. I thought I'd compromise today in honor of meeting you for the first time, but maybe we should stick with the normal set of rules—"

"No, no," May interrupted, "I'll put the dishes away." She sighed and rolled her eyes. "Come on D.J.; it'll just take me a few minutes." She led her friend into the kitchen.

"There's the dutiful daughter I know and love!" May's mom called after them. "There's carrots, nuts, apples, and bananas in there, too, if you're looking for a snack."

After quickly putting the dishes away and preparing a snack for both of them, May led D.J. down some stairs to a room that looked like a second living room. A sofa and various plush chairs surrounded a large-screen TV on the wall. May directed D.J. to the sofa and began powering equipment on and grabbing a controller.

May quickly explained the various buttons on the controller, then turned on the Overwatch game and entered a chat room where Lexi and Payton waited. D.J. was thoroughly confused. With so many joysticks and buttons, she knew she'd never be able to keep them all straight.

"Hey, ladies!" May called out.

"Hey, May! Is D.J. with you?" Lexi's could be heard from the speakers surrounding the sofa.

"Go ahead. Say hi!" May encouraged.

"Uh...hi guys!" D.J. called out.

"OMG, I'm so excited to play with you; this is gonna be awesome!" Lexi squealed.

"Hey," Payton greeted in the monotone voice D.J. was getting used to "Okay; since you're new to this game and there are three of us, we are going to do a 3 v. deathmatch."

"Got it!" confirmed Lexi.

"Uh...what's a 3 v. 3—" D.J. began but May interrupted her.

"Oooo! 3 v. 3 deathmatch! Good idea, Pay!" May took the controller from D.J. and pushed a few buttons. "We're all set; we're in the queue—in line to join a game. You, Lex, and Pay will be in a match against a team of three other players."

"Okay...so...like...what do I do?" asked D.J., feeling overwhelmed and completely out of her element.

"Well, first you choose a character," May instructed. "Just use the left joystick and pick a character, any character."

"Um...How about her?"

"Symmetra?" asked May.

"No, no, no! She's not good for this game mode!" Lexi cautioned.

"Uh...How about her?"

"Mercy? Sure," May approved.

"That'll work," agreed Payton. "Mercy's good at healing."

D.J. had no idea what that meant. She hoped it would become clear as the game went on. Those hopes were dashed moments later, however, when the match started.

May began rapid-fire instructions. "The left joystick makes you move. You shoot by pressing the 'RT' and jump by pressing 'A'. And each character has different abilities. As you can see, on the bottom right corner it says what button you press to use your abilities."

"Wait. Can we pause for a minute, so I can figure this out a little better?" D.J. asked May.

"No, there's no pausing in this game, and if you leave the match before it's over you can get banned from playing again."

"Seriously? But what if you have to go to the bathroom or your phone rings or your mom asks you to do something?"

"Nope. No pausing. That stuff just has to wait," May explained.

D.J. was trying to figure out what buttons to push but couldn't concentrate because she was also trying to follow Payton's orders.

"Shoot the characters with the red outline!" Payton yelled. "Press the right 'D' pad to bring out your pistol, then you can use your 'Ult' to fly and 'RT' to shoot them. But you can only use your 'Ult' when you're at full percentage, so make sure of that first."

Lexi notified everyone that she wanted to get some health packs but was having trouble because the other team's Sombra had hacked them. D.J.'s head swam, with all of her senses on overload. The screen seemed to have twelve different things going on at the same time. She had no idea what to focus in on. The controller felt like it had fifty buttons. How could she remember eighty different combinations of buttons to get her character to do anything on the screen? If that weren't enough, she had Payton barking out orders, Lexi providing commentary on her own mission, and May jumping up and down next to her on the sofa, cheering them all on.

The match ended after about five minutes, but it felt like an hour to D.J. Every muscle in her body had tensed with the stress of trying not to let her team down. May hugged her; somehow, they had won the match. She had no idea how that happened.

D.J. thanked May, then suggested May take over with the game so she could just watch and try to learn more about it as a spectator. May readily agreed, grabbing the controller from D.J.'s hand, and D.J. sat back with a deep sigh of relief.

* * *

"Sooo?" Persephone prompted excitedly.

"So, what?" asked D.J.

"Did you ask your cute guy to the dance?"

"Oh...no. I almost did, but...I was just too nervous."

"That's too bad. Maybe tomorrow. How was the rest of your day?" Persephone quizzed while transplanting a small azalea bush.

"I don't know." D.J. thought back on the events of the day. "Pretty good, I guess."

"Pretty good? Why not great?"

"There were some great times, like when I learned that Mr. Steele leads a 4-H group for gardeners. I'm really excited about it." D.J. smiled as she spun a morning glory bloom back and forth through her fingers, appreciating the contrast between the deep indigo of the outer petals and the fuchsia and light pink closer to the center of the flower.

"I can't think of anything more exciting and wonderful!" exclaimed Persephone. "So, with great news like that, what made today just 'pretty good'?"

"You're right; I guess it was a good day. I mean...I also had a play date with my new friends, so...yeah, it was a good day."

"Oh, how fun!" Persephone flashed her a warm smile. "So...why the sad note to your voice?"

"Well, my friends May, Payton, and Lexi are great and all; I'm really happy and thankful to have gotten to know them, but..." D.J. sighed deeply as she searched for the words. "I really like *them*; they're really cool and nice and everything. I just don't feel like I have a ton in common with them, know what I mean? Dad says I should ask them to do stuff I like to do, but I'm afraid I'll scare them away or something. I can see why Dad said that, but I think it would be easier to just do stuff that they all like to do and...who knows? Maybe I'll start liking what they like."

"Hmmm..." Persephone nodded knowingly. "Daisy, I didn't tell you the complete story about my marriage. Remember how Hades stole me away to the Underworld?"

D.J. nodded, "Yeah—when he kidnapped you. I can't even imagine; how *scary!*"

"I *was* scared," Persephone admitted, "and I don't regret my fear—that was natural in such a situation. What I regret is my reaction. I just sat back and let it happen. When we got to the Underworld I didn't fight back. I thought it would be useless, so I didn't even try. I don't know if I could have gotten myself free or not, but I didn't even *try*. I just sat there all depressed and feeling sorry for myself."

She shook her head with disgust as she watered the azalea plant in its new home.

"But then your dad ordered Hades to release you, so it all ended up okay anyway, right?" D.J. asked.

"Not really. Hades *really* didn't want to let me go, so he tried to get off on a technicality. He tricked me."

D.J. cocked her head to the side and scrunched her eyebrows in confusion.

"Well, Hades didn't like seeing me so sad, so he started coming to my part of the Underworld palace trying to cheer me up. I think that all started even before my dad demanded Hades let me go. He was being all nice and funny and caring—you know, all the things he should have been *before* he kidnapped me! But one day he was being particularly charming, and he offered me some pomegranate seeds."

"OMG, I love pomegranates!"

"I know, right? They're *amazing*! Anyway, I ate six pomegranate seeds," Persephone admitted with a sigh and another disgusted shake of her head.

"I don't get it," D.J. said. "First of all, how did you stop at six? I would have devoured the whole thing! And secondly...like, what's the big deal with eating pomegranate seeds?"

Persephone threw her head back and groaned toward the sky. "See, there's this stupid little *rule*. If you eat something in the Underworld you can't leave."

D.J. gasped.

"Yeah, well...at first that wasn't a problem for me. For months I had been too depressed to eat or drink anyway."

"*Months?*" D.J. exclaimed. "I can't even make it from lunch until dinner without a snack!"

"But that day was different. Hades had been super-nice for weeks and—yeah, I admit it; I was feeling pretty hungry and even more thirsty, so...I don't know. I just got all caught up in the moment, imagining the tart little burst of pomegranate juice on my tongue and how it might add some much-needed hydration to my super-dry mouth...and I ate the seeds. I mean...

it was *six little seeds!* Who would have thought that would count?"

"Seriously!" D.J. agreed, "That definitely shouldn't have been enough to count under the rules!"

"Well, it was." Persephone sighed. Then she looked at D.J. straight in the eye and said, "But that's when it hit me."

"When what hit you?"

"The courage to stand up for myself. I had just sat there and taken it when he stole me, but I was *not* going to do that again!"

"So, what did you do?"

"First, I gave Hades a piece of my mind. Loudly. I told him he can't be all nice and romantic, caring and gentlemanly while *tricking me* at the *same time*. I told him I understood that he was lonely. I really got it. I mean, who wouldn't be? It's all dreary and depressing down there and he was completely alone for years. It's probably why his manners were so atrocious. Anyway, I told him I didn't mind spending some time with him, but I deserved to spend *some* time in the world above, too.

Surprisingly, he agreed. So now I spend six months of every year up here and six months down there."

"Six *months?*"

"Yeah. It's not so bad, I guess," Persephone said with a shrug.

"What do you do down there?" D.J. asked.

"Not much! I wish I could garden down there, but...no sun, of course. Hades mostly plays video games. I spend time thinking about what I want to add to my garden when I can come back up."

"OMG, video games are what my friends do, too! They're *totally* into them and I'm totally...not."

"Yeah, Hades is into shooting games... *Doom, Destiny*...those types. He wanted me to play with him, but I just couldn't get into it. He felt bad, so he went out and got me a game called *Plants vs. Zombies*. For a video game, it's not half bad; I actually have fun playing it." Persephone giggled.

"Huh. I'll have to ask May if she has that game; maybe I can play *that* with them instead of *Overwatch*."

"Oh, *Overwatch*? Hades plays that one, and I can never figure out what's going on; I'm always confused."

"I know, right?" D.J. exclaimed, "I just played one match and that was more than enough for me!"

"Daisy, you need to stand up for yourself. If these girls are really your friends, they'll do things that you like, too. I mean, if I can get Hades to compromise, you should be able to get your friends to meet you halfway, too."

"Man, have you been talking with my dad? That's pretty much what he said."

"Well, your dad is a very smart man, then!" Persephone smiled. "Talk to your friends. I'm sure they'll understand."

"We'll see," D.J. said, adding a nervous sigh.

Chapter VII

Was there some sort of conspiracy against her? First, her dad. Then Persephone. Now it was Ms. Peters offering a whole lesson on self-advocacy. "Stand up for yourself; Yes, I *get it!*" D.J. felt like yelling. Ms. Peters was focusing on the benefits of self-advocacy and the consequences of not standing up for yourself, but she left out the most important part—the one about how you're supposed to find the courage to do it!

She discreetly looked over at Lexi in the seat next to her and tried to imagine a way to break it to her friends that she would appreciate doing other things with them. She just couldn't come up with something that would guarantee the girls wouldn't turn their backs on her, and she feared taking any chances with her fragile, new friendships.

Later, in her Language Arts class, D.J. was excited to learn the Greek mythology lesson for the day included Hades and Persephone. She thought back on all her amazing dreams of late that featured the beautiful goddess. Actually, everything in her told D.J. that her time with Persephone was *not* time spent dreaming. She couldn't explain it, but she just knew it was something different. She thought it would be best to keep her relationship with Persephone to herself, though; nobody would believe her if she spoke of it.

Regardless of how she was meeting with Persephone, it saddened D.J. again to think about such a kind, nurturing, happy person being bullied into a marriage and tricked into living somewhere she didn't want to be. D.J. got lost in the memories of her conversations with Persephone, and suddenly an idea began to take hold—one that could both verify her belief and help a friend.

Hudson startled her, tapping her on the shoulder. "You okay?" he asked with concern in his voice.

"Uh...yeah, why?"

"The bell rang. It's time to go."

"Oh! Thanks," D.J. said, her face flush with embarrassment. "Sorry; I was just thinking about something."

"Yeah, I kinda figured that out," he said with a teasing smirk.

D.J. smiled and gathered her books. "Don't laugh at me!" she demanded, good-naturedly.

"Wouldn't dream of it." He laughed as he started toward the door. "I'll see you in science."

Lunchtime found the girls, once again, comparing notes about their gaming session from the night before. D.J. didn't feel quite so left out, since she had some inkling of what they were talking about. It was far from her favorite conversation topic, but at least she was part of it.

"You're coming over again today, right Deej?" May asked.

"Yeah. Dad said I could, as long as I'm home by six."

"Awesome! Now that you're more familiar with the game, we can try another mission or two with you actually playing."

"Oh, that's okay; I don't mind watching you guys play," D.J. was quick to assure May. "Although," she added, "do you happen to have a game called *Plants vs. Zombies?*"

"Umm...yeah; I think I still have that game," May said. "Have you played it before?"

"No, but I've heard it's fun. I wouldn't mind trying it today—if you don't mind."

"Not at all!" May exclaimed with a bright smile. "And that's a game that the two of us will be able to play together, so that will be awesome!"

* * *

"How was school today, sweetie?" asked Dad as he sprinkled parmesan cheese onto his plate of the spaghetti that D.J. had helped him make for dinner.

"Good," answered D.J. "I think I did pretty well on the math quiz. I also got my latest lab report in science back, and I got an A."

"Fantastic! And what did you and May do this afternoon?"

"Just some video games."

"Hmmm...another day of video games, huh?" Dad pushed further.

"Yeah. This time May and I played a game together instead of teaming up with Payton and Lexi. We played *Plants vs. Zombies.* For a video game it wasn't too bad; it was actually kinda fun."

"Oh good," Dad said with a smile. "Does that mean you talked with her about compromising on activities?

"No, not yet. I'm still trying to work up the courage to talk to the girls about that," D.J. confessed, "but I'm getting closer."

"Well, it's encouraging that May agreed to play a game you enjoyed more," Dad offered optimistically. "Maybe that's a sign the girls are more open to new ideas than you've given them credit for."

"Maybe," D.J. conceded. Anxious to change the subject, she decided to take a chance at moving forward with the plan she had devised in her Language Arts class. "Dad, do we still have Mom's greenhouse gear? Did we move it all here?"

"Some of it. We couldn't bring the bigger things, so we left those for the new greenhouse owners, but we have most of the smaller items. Why?"

"I'm working on a planting project. Where can I find that stuff?"

"In the attic," Dad answered. "There's three or four boxes you can look through to the left of the stairs. Let me know if you can't find what you're looking for, though."

"Thanks, Dad! I'll go check it out after I do dinner clean-up," D.J. said with a smile.

* * *

D.J. excitedly prepared for bed. Climbing under the covers, she carefully placed Fern next to her, along with what she had retrieved from the box in the attic. Then she took a deep breath and opened the Greek mythology book that had accompanied her to bed for three nights in a row.

After reading a fascinating chapter about Aphrodite and Hephaistos, D.J. was pleased and relieved to find herself sitting on the stone bench under the now-familiar weeping willow tree. And her experiment had paid off! Fern and the item from the attic were sitting next to her. Standing up, she took a deep, appreciative breath of the sweetly perfumed air, and she marveled again at the gorgeous garden surrounding her. "Persephone?" she called out.

In a blink, her environment completely changed. She braced her legs and threw out her arms in surprise. She was standing beside her new friend, who was sitting on a stone bench. It looked similar to the bench D.J. had just been sitting on, but the weeping willow and the garden she had been admiring had disappeared.

Now they were in the largest field of tulips—or of anything, for that matter—that D.J. had ever seen. Massive stripes of tulips formed a rainbow, beginning with the striking purple that surrounded them, and ending with bands of stunning orange, then deep, magnificent red against the horizon.

"Hi, Daisy!" Persephone smiled up at her. She scooted to the side of the bench and patted the space next to her. "Come sit. This is one of my favorite places to be this time of year. Amazing, isn't it?"

"It's...breathtaking!" D.J. agreed in awe. "I've never seen so many flowers all in one place! And the colors are so brilliant, and there's so *many* colors!"

"I think the purple are my favorite, but I struggle to decide between these darker ones around us and the lighter, lilac-colored ones just up ahead," Persephone shared. "Or, at least, these are my favorite this year. Last year I was really taken with the various shades of pink."

"Man," D.J. said, shaking her head. "I don't think I could choose. They're all just so beautiful, and they look so spectacular together, know what I mean?"

"I do. Planting the bulbs just before heading back to the Underworld every year always offers me hope and excitement for how it will look when they grace us with their majesty in the spring."

They sat in companionable silence for some time, both soaking in the wonder and beauty of the sight before them. Eventually, Persephone asked, "So, do you officially have a date to the Spring Fling yet?"

"No," D.J. admitted. "I'm still trying to decide if I want to ask him. I mean...it would be okay if I just went by myself, right? I'd still have fun."

"Hmmm...sounds like you're trying to talk yourself into not having to face your fear," Persephone said with a teasing smile.

"I don't fear asking him. I just...I don't know. I get in front of him and I get too embarrassed to ask something like that," D.J. tried to explain.

"Let me guess. You haven't talked to your friends yet about your lack of love for video games, either, right?"

"No, but that's actually what I wanted to talk to you about today." D.J. turned her body to face Persephone more directly.

"Oh, really?" Persephone asked, eyebrows raised in interest.

"Yes. I was thinking today about what you, Dad, and even Ms. Peters have been saying about standing up for yourself. I was also thinking about everything you've told me about your life with Hades." D.J. paused for a moment, looking down next to her on the bench. "Oh, actually—can we go back to the bench I was on when I got here?"

Almost before she was able to complete her request, D.J. found herself suddenly shaded by the grand weeping willow. Persephone sat on the bench to her left, Fern to her right. "Okay, can I just say? That is *So. Cool*," she gushed over their magical mode of transportation.

"It comes in handy when you have a large garden to tend to," explained Persephone with a smile.

"I guess it would." D.J. cleared her throat, wanting to get back to what she had begun to say in the tulip field. "Anyway, I was thinking that I need to talk to my friends, like you've told me."

Persephone nodded encouragingly.

"I'm still a little nervous about doing it," continued D.J., "so I have a challenge for you. I will talk to May, Payton, and Lexi about wanting to try doing something other than video games—*if* you stand up for yourself, too."

"Me? What do you mean?"

"Well, you said that for half the year you're stuck down in the Underworld where it's dark and dreary. That's no good for you! You need green! You need growth, life, and beauty! You need to talk to Hades and demand that he allows you to keep house plants around the castle. There's no sunlight down there but there are ways around that." D.J. grabbed the item she had gotten from the attic. "My mom used a bunch of these grow lights for many of her seedlings and some of her indoor plants, too, like her beautiful peace lilies. Also, some houseplants are shade-loving and don't need a lot of light, so I think they'd work really well in your situation. And one of the best plants like that is..." D.J. reached around and grabbed her longtime friend, "Fern, here. She has been a great friend to me for as long as I can remember, and I can think of no better houseplant to begin your indoor garden. Besides, she's just so beautiful, there's no way Hades will ever be able to deny you when you tell him you want houseplants!" D.J. looked up from Fern, surprised to find tears in Persephone's eyes.

"Oh, Daisy," Persephone whispered, "I don't even know what to say! I know how important Fern has been to you over the years, and I would be absolutely honored to take over her care!" She threw her arms around D.J., nearly smothering her in a huge hug. "And you're right," she continued as she pulled back to look D.J. in the eye, "I've never even thought to insist that Hades allow houseplants in the castle; I guess I just assumed nothing like that could ever come to be. But this is a brilliant idea and I think it'll work!"

D.J. felt her smile through her entire body, all warm and sparkly. It felt incredible to think that someone like her could help someone as amazing as Persephone. Better yet—just as she had hoped—she was inspired to stand up for herself. If she got nervous or embarrassed, she would just think of Persephone doing the very same thing. How bad could standing up to her friends be? At least she didn't have to stand up to the God of the Underworld!

Chapter VIII

D.J. made her way to the school cafeteria lunch table with determination. She found Lexi and Payton in a heated debate as she sat down next to May.

"No way!" Lexi argued passionately. "*Widowmaker* is *obviously* the better sniper! She has that sweet scope!"

"Yeah, but Hanzo can climb walls and has scatter arrow!" Payton countered with equal conviction. "There's no *way* a scope can compete with that!"

"Don't mind them." May dismissed the dispute with a roll of her eyes as she turned her attention to D.J. "They go on like this for hours sometimes. So...any plans for the weekend?"

"Um..." D.J. took a deep, fortifying breath. "Actually, I was wondering if you girls would all like to come over and hang out at my house tomorrow." Lexi and Payton stopped their good-natured bickering to look over at D.J.

"I have to get my chores done in the morning," May said, "but I should be done by lunchtime, so that sounds fun for the afternoon. Pay? Lex? How about you guys?"

"Yeah, I don't think we have any plans," Lexi agreed. "If you just write down your address for me, I'll ask my mom to drive me over after lunch."

All eyes turned to Payton. "Sure," she said with a half shrug. "What do you want to do?"

D.J. smiled brightly and sighed with relief. "I have some fun things in mind, and my dad said he'd order pizza for us and take everyone home after dinner if you guys could come over."

"Pizza's always good," said Payton with an approving nod.

"Awesome," D.J. cheered as she grabbed a notebook out of her backpack. "Let me just write down your numbers so I can call you all tonight and make sure it's okay with your parents."

* * *

D.J. entered Mr. Steele's science class feeling equally excited and nervous. She was happy and relieved that her friends hadn't declined her invitation from the get-go, but she worried that when they got to her house they'd change their minds and immediately want to turn around and go back home.

"What's up?" Hudson asked as she sat in her seat at their table. "You look like you're stressed out or something."

"Oh, it's nothing," D.J. dismissed with a shake of her head and a swipe of her hand through the air, as if she were pushing aside her concerns. "I invited the girls over to my house tomorrow, and I'm just hoping they'll have fun enough to want to come back sometime."

"I'm sure they will," he assured with a smile. "What are you going to do while they're there?"

"Um...I have a gardening project in mind."

"Gardening, huh? You're really into that, aren't you? That's what Mr. Steele's 4-H group is all about, right?"

"Yeah. Gardening is awesome. There's the fun in the planning, the challenge in creating a habitat that's just right for each plant, the wonder of watching them grow, and the pride when you see them fully grown and get to pick them for a bouquet or eat them for dinner," she explained.

"Wow. You make it actually sound fun!" he praised. "And you said the 4-H meetings are on Tuesdays?"

"Yeah," she said. "Did you want to go, too?" D.J. nearly slapped her hand over her mouth when she realized she had just asked Hudson out...kinda...so to speak... in a way...but not really...

"Hmmm." He looked up at the ceiling as if making a big decision. He looked at D.J., who was staring back with wide eyes, sweating in her nervousness and hoping she wouldn't throw up her lunch. "I don't know..." He drew out the last word dramatically. "That would really be putting my life on the line...all that time with Sinister Steele. There'll probably be blunt and sharp objects that he could murder us all with, too! Soooo... tell ya what. I'll risk my *very life* and try this 4-H gardening thing with you...*if* you go to my soccer game on Sunday. It's at noon and it's a home game, so it'll just be over at the park; will you be free?"

D.J. smiled and breathed a sigh of relief. "I'm free on Sunday. Yeah; watching your game would be fun!" Then she decided to throw all caution to the wind and go for broke. "Actually, I've been meaning to ask you— are you planning to go to the Spring Fling dance next Friday?"

"I hadn't decided yet."

"Well...I was thinking of going. Wanna... go with me?" D.J. squeaked out the question, then held her breath again, wincing in preparation for a big let-down.

"Sure," he said with a smile.

Before D.J. could even register the fact that she had just asked a boy to

a dance—and that he had said yes—
Mr. Steele bellowed, *"I can make your
hands clap!"*

D.J. found herself pulled into the com-
pulsion to join the students in their
answering *clap-clap-clap-clap-clap* to
the rhythm of the popular song by the
same title.

"Okay, let's get down to business,"
Mr. Steele said calmly in the now-silent
room.

D.J. snuck one final smile over at Hudson
before focusing on taking her experiment
notes out of her backpack.

* * *

"I propose we go out for ice cream after
dinner in celebration," Dad casually commented as he prepared a taco from the
fixings D.J. had helped him put together
for dinner.

"In celebration of what?" D.J. asked,
confused, as she slid the bowl of chopped
tomatoes toward herself. "Not that I'm
refusing, of course!"

"Well, you're standing here in front of me, hale and hearty. You've successfully survived an *entire week* at the school you *begged* me not to make you go to. I'd say that's as good a reason for ice cream as any I can think of!" Dad said with a wink in her direction.

"Daaa-aaad," D.J. drawled with a sigh and a roll of her eyes.

Dad chuckled. "How did your invitation to your friends go over today? Should I be prepared to receive guests tomorrow?"

"Um-hm." D.J. nodded around a big bite of her taco. "All of their parents were okay with them coming over. It looks like about one in the afternoon. Do you mind if we stop by the garden-supply store and the arts-and-crafts store when we go out for ice cream tonight? There's a few things I want to get so we'll be all prepared for a fun project."

"Sure," Dad agreed with a smile as he got up to make himself a second taco.

"Oh, and Dad? Do you mind if I go to the park on Sunday...say...around...noon?"

"I don't see why not. What's going on at the park?"

"Oh, just a soccer game." D.J. tried to sound as casual as she could."I thought... you know...it might be fun to...watch it."

Dad shot her a strange look and studied her for a moment.

D.J. took another bite of her taco and looked intently at the table.

"Soccer, huh? Tell me, what has prompted this plan to peruse the pitch?"

"The what?" D.J. scowled in confusion, thrown off by Dad's weird language.

"The pitch. That's what football is played on."

"No, Dad." D.J. sighed and shook her head in frustration. "Not football—*soccer*...on the *field*...at the *park*. Can I go?"

Dad chuckled. D.J. couldn't understand what was so funny. "Sweetheart, football is what soccer is called everywhere but the United States, and a 'pitch' is the name for the field the game is played on."

"Oh."

"So, I'm guessing you haven't become an overnight fan of the sport, which leads me to believe it's a certain soccer *player* you've taken an interest in. Would you like to share a little about this athlete you've suddenly decided to become so supportive of?" Dad flashed a mischievous sparkle in his eyes.

"No, Dad!" She clicked her tongue and breathed out a dramatic sigh as if to scold him for such silly thoughts. "It's not like that!" she continued emphatically. "A friend from school asked me, so I said yes...because—you know—I wanted to be...supportive and uh...a good...classmate. That's all," she explained with a dismissive shrug of her shoulders. She looked across the room, suddenly feeling uncomfortable with direct eye contact. She hoped Dad didn't notice her blushing.

"Well wasn't that nice of you!" Dad exclaimed as he took his empty plate to the sink. "Is this classmate someone you also plan to see at the Spring Fling next week?"

"What—when—who—how...how do you know about Spring Fling?" D.J. sputtered in a panic, wondering if her dad had a spy planted in her school...or had he somehow learned to read her mind?

Dad laughed heartily as he walked toward the living room. "That's my job, kiddo. It's just what I do." He looked back over his shoulder and winked, then turned with another laugh and walked on.

D.J. slumped in her seat and groaned into her hands.

Chapter IX

D.J. nervously reorganized the supplies on the picnic table in their small backyard. It was a beautiful, warm, and sunny spring day, so at least she didn't have to worry about rain. She had enough other concerns on her mind. She worried she had made a big mistake in asking her friends over. Her mind spun with dozens of what-ifs. What if the girls took one look at what she wanted to do and walked straight back out the door? What if they stayed—to be polite—but hated it and all agreed never to come back again? What if they laughed at her for her idea of a fun afternoon? What if they decided that maybe she wasn't a good friend to have, after all, and started ignoring her at school?

Trying to shake off her negative thoughts, she made her way to the front yard to meet the girls as they arrived. It wasn't long before they were all there, chatting and giggling as she led them into her house for a tour and introductions to her dad.

"Well, hello, ladies!" greeted Dad as he held the front door open for them. "It's very nice to meet you all! If you need anything, I'll be in my office. Otherwise, I'll leave you girls to do your own thing. Help yourselves to the snacks that are on the counter. There's also lemonade in the fridge."

The quick tour of the house started with the kitchen and continued on up to D.J.'s room.

May asked, "What are these tiny little grass-like things over here by the window?"

"Oh, those are some daisies and pansies." D.J. beamed with pride. "I planted them earlier this week, so they're just starting to make their way in the world. It won't take them long to start looking like the beautiful flowers they are, though, and then I can transplant them to the flower beds out in the yard. Come on!"

D.J. led them back downstairs to the living room on the way out to the backyard. She carried a bag of pretzels, the container of lemonade, and four cups so they'd be able to snack through their project.

Payton came to a sudden halt as they entered the living room, though. The rest of the girls nearly bumped into her as they attempted to stop. "Wait," Payton said as she looked around the room, "Where's your TV?"

"Hmm?" D.J. asked, as she turned to look, confused for a moment.

"Where. Is. Your. Television?" Payton asked clearly and slowly in a disturbingly serious tone.

"Oh, uh...yeah, we...we don't have one."

"Wait." Lexi chimed in, "What do you mean? You said you don't have an Xbox, but you didn't say anything about not having a *TV!*"

"Well...you never asked about it and we've never had one, so I guess I didn't think to mention it." D.J. wondered what the big deal was.

The girls stared at her.

Lexi chuckled nervously as she attempted to break the uncomfortable silence. "Hey, did you know that the first president to be televised was Franklin D. Roosevelt?"

"Lex, enough with the trivia. This is serious," scolded May with a roll of her eyes. She turned back to D.J. "So, like...*never*. You *never* had one?" She was incredulous. "How could you *never* have a TV? Like...what do you *do*?"

"I don't know." D.J. was starting to wilt under the weight of anxious embarrassment. "If you've never had one, I guess you don't miss it," she explained with a half shrug.

"Well, what are we going to do today?" blurted Payton.

D.J. could almost hear the girls silently asking one another, *How long did we agree to be here?* as they looked among themselves in a panic.

Throwing on her brightest smile, she tamped down her own worry that they would bolt for the front door. "Actually, I was just about to show you what I thought we could do today. Come on!" She waved toward the door that led to the backyard.

Outside, D.J. set the snack supplies on a corner of the picnic table. The girls were following her, so they hadn't run away, but they wore much more somber faces and moved considerably slower as they joined her and looked over the supplies laid out before them. She realized that this was her moment of truth. The girls were one disappointment away from coming up with excuses to go home early. Would they give her a chance to share her favorite joy with them?

There was only one way to find out. With a determined, fortifying breath she explained, "I thought it might be neat if we all had matching flower pots to put on our front porches or near our front doors. Well...not matching, exactly. Similar. I got these plain terra cotta pots, but I got these paints and stencils, so we can decorate them however we want. Then I got this potting soil and these impatiens, geraniums, peonies, and petunias so we can arrange and plant the flowers we want; however we want." She held her breath, awaiting their response.

May took a quick, assessing look at the other girls, apparently judging their level of interest. D.J. noticed that Payton had a rather doubtful expression, but either May missed it, or she didn't care. "Sure," she said for all of them. "Sounds fun!"

The other girls shrugged and nodded their agreement as they each chose a seat at the table and grabbed a pot to decorate. D.J. nearly wept with relief as they began squabbling good-naturedly over who got to use which color of paint first.

"Lex, I'm oldest, so obviously I get first choice on color. I'll be taking that green, thank you!" demanded Payton as she reached for the paint.

"No way, old lady! I called dibs right before we sat down. The green is All. Mine." Lexi grabbed for it a second too late, so Payton snatched it away.

"Ha! You'll just be green with envy while you're watching me paint my pretty green background," taunted Payton.

Lexi stuck her tongue out at Payton and made a raspberry sound as she grabbed the yellow paint. "Did you know green is a symbol of fertility?" she quizzed. "That's why it was 'the thing' to wear green wedding gowns in the 1400's."

"How do you do that?" asked May as she poured some pink paint in a bowl. "How do you always have some weird, obscure trivial fact about...*everything?*"

"It's not really about *everything,*" Lexi explained. "Just about historical stuff. Mom is a history professor at the UW, and dinnertime for us always includes historical trivia games. It's kinda fun." She shrugged.

"Wait. Your mom works at the University of Washington?" Payton asked, impressed.

"Yeah...why?"

"It's just...I've dreamed my whole life of going to the UW. I've never known anyone who actually teaches there."

"Why have you always wanted to go to the UW?" D.J. asked Payton. "I actually thought about maybe going to WSU."

Payton gasped dramatically as she reared her head back in what D.J. hoped was only mock disgust. "Bite your tongue! We Huskies *spit* upon the lowly Cougars of Washington State University! There's no comparison; obviously UW is the best school! My mom and dad both went there. My room was decorated in purple and gold before I was even born!"

May began to laugh. "Can you imagine what your parents would say, Pay, if you went home and told them that after thinking long and hard, you've decided you want to be a Coug?"

"OMG, they'd probably kick me out and disown me," Payton said, chuckling. "I should do it, just to mess with them."

"You are so cruel!" said Lexi, laughing.

"What are you talking about? 'Sweet-And-Innocent' is my middle name!"

"More like 'Twisted-And-Evil'." May laughed. "What *is* your middle name, by the way?"

"Savannah. What's yours?" Payton asked May.

"Ooo...that's pretty. Mine is Clair. How about yours, Lex?"

"Actually, Lexi is kinda part of my middle name, Alejandra. My mom insisted on naming me after her mother, Maria, but I don't think my dad has ever really been a fan of my abuela, because he started calling me by my middle name the day I was born and it just kinda stuck. How about you, D.J.? Wait...what does D.J. even stand for?"

"Oh...it's the initials of my first and middle name, but...I've always been a little... sensitive about my first name, so I started going by D.J. when I started kindergarten. My dad told me that my mom wanted to name me Daisy, after her favorite flower, and he wanted to name me Jane, after his favorite person (my mom), so...that's what they did." She shrugged one shoulder self-consciously. "Daisy Jane."

"Awww...that's beautiful!" gushed May, bringing her hand to her chest in sincerity. "And that is So. Sweet! about your dad! OMG, how romantic! Oh, I want to call you Daisy now! And there's no need to be awkward about it, silly; it's a *magnificent* name—your mom was *totally* right to want to name you that! Wait, where is your mom? We only met your dad when we got here," asked May.

"Oh, she, um...she...passed away in September," D.J. admitted uncomfortably.

After a flurry of gasps, "OMG's", "Oh no's" and "I'm so sorry's", Lexi quietly asked the question on all the girls' minds. "What happened?"

"She had cancer. Pancreatic cancer. She fought really, really hard, but...it was just too much," D.J. explained with a sorrowful shake of her head. "Toward the end, she was always in massive amounts of pain, no matter how much medicine we gave her. She tried to be brave around me, but...I could tell she was hurting. It was *so hard* to see her hurting. ...Dad and I are still trying to get used to life without Mom here with us. We miss her like crazy, but...we're also relieved to know that at least she's not in pain anymore."

All three of D.J.'s friends dropped their brushes, ran over, and enveloped her in a big hug.

It was always hard to talk about her mom, but she felt better, having told the girls about her. "Thanks," she said, meeting the eyes of each. Trying to brighten the mood, she added, "It's actually my mom who taught me to love gardening so much. She was an *ah-MA-zing* gardener! She grew plants and flowers in her greenhouses that were sold at all sorts of nurseries, gardening stores, and flower shops around the county."

"That's awesome," Lexi commented, as the girls went back to their painting. "I never even thought about where the plants at the store come from."

"Yeah, we were always busiest around this time of year when a lot of people are buying plants and flowers for their gardens."

"I hadn't really thought about gardening," admitted Payton, "but I wouldn't mind trying it; it sounds fun."

D.J. told them about the Tuesday 4-H meetings. "They help the community and they compete with other 4-H groups," she explained. "If any of you want to join me, I know Dad wouldn't mind giving you rides."

Another flurry of activity circled the group, this time of nodding heads and affirmative statements like "Yeah", "That sounds cool", and "That sounds fun" said enthusiastically. May finished off with, "I'll join this 4-H group thingy if you let me call you Daisy whenever we're doing anything garden-related."

D.J. laughed. "Deal. This is awesome; I'm so psyched!" D.J. beamed, anxious and excited to go to the first meeting with all her friends.

"Where are the meetings held?" asked Payton.

"Mr. Steele's house. He started the group when his kids got interested in gardening.

"Hold on. Soul Sucking Steele is involved in this thing?" Payton looked horrified.

Lexi grimaced and added, "And there are Spawn of Steele? That's just cringe-y!"

"Stop! You guys are terrible." D.J. laughed with a shake of her head. "Why are you always so hard on Mr. Steele? I was so scared to go to his class on Monday after hearing all you guys said about him at lunch that day!"

"I don't know—" May shrugged. "We've never had him. Just heard about him."

"Well you heard wrong! He's actually pretty nice and he's even funny sometimes!"

"Huh! Never would have guessed," said Payton.

"Come with me on Tuesday. You'll see!" encouraged D.J. "Actually," she added on a whim, "Hudson said he's going, too."

"Hudson Alexander?" May asked, looking shocked.

"Yep," D.J. answered, smiling. "He said he'd go if I went to his soccer game at the park tomorrow afternoon."

Lexi squealed and jumped up from her seat. "OMG, he's *into* you! Did he ask you to be his girlfriend? I mean, asking you to go to watch him play is *pretty* serious!"

"No," D.J. admitted, "but he said he'd go to the Spring Fling with me next Friday!"

"No *way!* Guurrrrl, you are on *fire!*" praised May. "You've been here all of a single week and you got a date to the dance before any of us!"

"Thanks." D.J.'s cheeks were burning.

"Come here." May jumped up from her seat. "We need to celebrate. Let's make a new Celebration High-Five!"

May proceeded to choreograph an intricate hand-slapping, fist-bumping, and butt-waggling high-five/handshake that ended with a do-si-do move, a "whoop-whoop", and jazz hands. D.J. felt honored to be part of the over-the-top-high-five club.

"Wait!" Lexi suddenly called with arms outstretched as if to physically make everyone stop. "What are you going to wear tomorrow when you go watch the game?"

"Oh yeah," said May, suddenly very serious, biting on her thumbnail with her brows furrowed in concentration.

"What?" D.J. asked on a giggle. "I don't know. Jeans and a t-shirt? It's just a soccer game; do people dress up to watch those? I've never been to one. Besides, Hudson will be playing; I'm sure he won't even see me in the crowd."

"Oh, honey," Payton said with her arms crossed across her chest and a roll of her eyes, "you clearly don't know how this thing works. Of *course* he's going to see you! He's going to be searching you out before the game even begins! He's going to check out everything about you—your clothes, your hair, the wattage of your smile—*everything*."

"Oh," D.J. said nervously. "I didn't realize. Maybe I shouldn't have agreed to go. What if he can tell right away that I don't know even the first thing about soccer? Like...I just learned last night that the field is called a 'pitch' and that most of the world calls the game 'football'. If I didn't even know what the sport is really called or the name of the grass they play it on, I can't even imagine how much *more* I don't know!"

"Don't worry," Lexi soothed. "We'll have you looking so good, he won't even remember he's there to play soccer, much less the proper terminology!"

The girls finished up their painting as discussion over soccer-game wardrobe and hair design continued. D.J. was growing so nerved up about how she'd look to Hudson that she was close to not going after all. Luckily, the conversation drifted to plotting and planning ways for May, Payton, and Lexi to ask boys to the dance as they took a short snack break.

Dad suddenly appeared. "Hey, ladies; how's it going out here? Wow, these flower pots are looking great!"

"Thanks, Dad!" D.J. smiled.

"Tell me what you'd like on your pizza, so I can order dinner."

"Wow. Already?" Payton asked with a shocked expression. "The time has flown by; it seems like we just stared painting a few minutes ago!"

The girls put in their pizza orders, and after putting potting soil in their newly decorated pots, D.J. taught her friends how to transplant the young plants in a way that would keep the roots happy and allow enough room for growth as they flourished in their new homes. The girls were just cleaning up when Dad announced that their dinner had arrived.

* * *

"Daisy Jane, you are positively *glowing*," Persephone admired as they sat comfortably in a field of bluebells, blowing fuzz from the dandelions they had just picked.

D.J.'s smile beamed even wider. "I know, right? Oh, Persephone, I've just had the *best* couple of days! I can't wait to tell you about it, but first I have to know: How did it go with Hades? Did he let you start an indoor garden?"

Persephone smiled almost as brightly as D.J. She stretched out on the grass amid the flowers with her eyes closed toward the bright sun shining down upon them. "It took some negotiation, but he finally came around." She giggled.

"Why? What did he say?" D.J. quizzed, lying down next to her friend.

"He didn't *say* it, but his list of ridiculous excuses against it made it clear he was worried that if I spent time tending to an indoor garden I'd be spending less time with him. The irony is that when we spend time together now, it's not like it's *quality* time. He's usually playing his games and I'm reading a book on the couch or rolling my eyes and huffing because I'm so freaking bored!"

"So how did you get him to agree?"

"I promised to play video games—of my choice, like *Plants vs. Zombies* or *Harvest Moon*—with him at least once every week if he won't object to my indoor garden." Persephone giggled again. "He made me promise to play at least *twice* every week. I made a big deal of acting all put out, like the price was *way* too much. What he didn't know was that I was actually willing to play games once a *day* in return for the chance to garden year-round. He thought he had pulled one over on me when, really, I walked away the total winner of that battle!"

"Ooo...clever!" D.J. praised. "Look at you, the master negotiator!"

"Thank you, again, for the suggestion, and for your incredibly kind donation of Fern. She's absolutely beautiful as the star of my budding indoor garden."

"I'm so glad that all worked out." D.J. clapped excitedly.

"Enough about that, though." Persephone sat up and rubbed her hands together. "I want details now! Did you ask the girls to do something with you other than gaming? Did you ask that boy to the dance?"

"Yes, and yes," D.J. confirmed. "It was awesome! I asked the girls over for a playdate, but I didn't specify anything about what we'd do. They knew I don't own a gaming system, though, so they had to know we wouldn't be playing video games. Anyway, when I got to the class I have with Hudson, he caught me nervously thinking about having the girls over. That started a conversation that turned into him offering to try the gardening club with me, inviting me to watch his soccer game at the park tomorrow, and agreeing to go to the dance together!"

"Shut. The. Front. Door! You were able to get all that in a single conversation? I bow down to you, milady, and bask in all of your glorious expertise with boys!" Persephone raised her arms above her head and began bowing from the waist as she spoke.

"Stop that!" D.J. laughed. "I'm no expert. He's just really nice and I think he felt a little sorry for me."

"Uh, no. 'A little sorry for you' would have been him turning you down nicely or *maybe* agreeing to go to the dance. But the 4-H club, the game invite, *and* the dance? Yeah, he's *totally* into you, girlfriend!"

"That's what Lexi said!"

"Well, your friend knows what she's talking about. Speaking of which, how did the playdate with the gals go?"

"It went great," D.J. admitted with a contented sigh. "I was really nervous in the beginning because they happened to notice that we don't have a television."

"Well, what's the big deal with that?"

"That's what I thought! But, I think I could have shown them a UFO sitting in the corner of my room and they would have been less freaked out than they were about no TV. I thought for sure they were going to bolt!"

"Oh no! What did you do?"

"Besides nearly throwing up from nerves and embarrassment? I just took them out where I had a planting project set up for us. Luckily the girls had a great time. Payton actually mentioned that she learned more about May and Lexi in that one afternoon than the whole rest of the time they had been friends. I guess when they're gaming they just discuss what's going on in the game, and when they're *not* gaming, they just talk about what they want to do in their next game."

"That's what I was saying about Hades. Time together with a video game demanding all your attention is *not* the same thing as spending *time* together, creating and nurturing something."

"Exactly! I hope there will be enough quiet time in the 4-H meetings for us to talk like we did today. It was really fun."

"That's awesome they're going!" Persephone smiled warmly. "I'm so proud of you, Daisy. Just a week ago, you were so nervous and scared. Now, just look at you! You have not just one, but three supportive friends—*four* if you count the cute boy who's totally into you."

D.J. dropped her head, blushing.

"You took your own life in your hands and reached out to find people with similar interests.You stood up for yourself. And you even encouraged me to stand up, too, when I didn't think to do it for myself. In just a few short days' time you've bloomed before my eyes into the bold and beautiful Daisy I knew you to be. I'm proud of you, your dad is proud of you...and I know your mom is proud, too."

D.J. peeked up at Persephone and smiled shyly through unshed tears.

Persephone pulled D.J. into a warm hug, then looked her in the eye. "It's my busy time of year, and your social calendar is filling up, so I'm going to say so long to you for now. Just know I'll always be watching over you—even when I'm down in the Underworld. If you ever want to come back for a visit or need to chat, just grab any mythology book. I'll be here."

D.J.'s heart clenched with panic. She hadn't known the goddess long, but they had grown so close! She couldn't imagine facing days that weren't preceded by magical nights with her new friend. What if she needed help or advice or...a pruning partner? She didn't want to say goodbye! It felt too much like the one she had struggled through with her mom.

As if Persephone read her mind, she added, "This is not goodbye, Daisy Jane. I'm always here for you."

D.J. took a deep breath, filled with hope. "Are you sure? It will be okay for me to visit again sometime soon?"

"Absolutely," Persephone assured as she pulled D.J. into another hug. "Anytime."

"Thank you, Persephone," D.J. said, "for everything. I'm so thankful for the opportunity to get to know you and for all your help."

Persephone offered her another dazzling smile before she leaned forward and kissed D.J. on the forehead. D.J. closed her eyes, soaking in the warmth and love surrounding her. When she opened her eyes again, she was back in her bed with her mythology book lying on her chest. The clock told her it was time to get up. She lay still a few minutes more, though, thinking back on her amazing trips to Persephone's garden. She smiled and switched her thoughts to the day ahead. She had a *date* today! Well, kind of... sort of...a little bit...in a way... She had to get ready! She threw her covers off and skipped excitedly over to her closet. This was going to be an *awesome* day and an ah-*ma*-zing week; she just *knew* it!

Epilogue

The girls were right. Hudson saw D.J. immediately when she showed up about a half hour before his game. D.J. had decided to be true to herself, so she just wore the jeans and t-shirt she had originally thought to wear. Hudson didn't seem to mind at all. He ran over and greeted her, introduced her to his dad, and joked with her for a few minutes before his coach called him over to warm up for the game.

D.J. *thought* the game went okay. She watched a lot of running up and down the field—oops...the pitch—but she found it confusing. At the end of the game, Hudson's team was the only one with a point showing on the scoreboard, so D.J. was confident they had done well. Hudson's dad surprised her by inviting her out for ice cream with them after the game. She couldn't wait to call the girls and tell them all about it when she got home.

Tuesday's 4-H meeting was awesome. They spent the hour planting a garden that would provide produce for a local food pantry. D.J. couldn't wait to see how many fruits and veggies they'd be able to donate by the end of the summer!

Hudson and the girls enjoyed themselves...as soon as they got over their fear that Mr. Steele would suddenly turn into a vampire or werewolf or something. Actually, they went from thinking he was scary to thinking he was out of his mind, when he demonstrated the official rain dance he called absolutely crucial for a bountiful harvest. He *insisted* it would only work if they all performed the dance together—in its entirety. So, they danced—despite feeling foolish—then were *mortified* when they realized the joke was on them. Of *course* there was no such thing as a rain dance; Mr. Steele had gotten them good! D.J. laughed and laughed. May turned it around, though, morphing it into an official group high-five/handshake that included the lawn mower, the sprinkler and the mashed potato.

Hudson met D.J. at the Spring Fling as promised and stayed with her and her friends. The gardening club group members were some of the first to get out on the dance floor, since they had gotten over any insecurities and embarrassment with "The Rain Dance Incident," as they had all come to call it. May showed off her boogie moves. Payton nearly started a riot when she told some eighth-grade boy that his dandruff was so bad the principal had to declare a snow day—after she caught him ruthlessly picking on a small sixth grade boy for having funny-looking hair. Lexi got her first kiss by none other than Bode McKenzie, who swore on his little brother's life that he hadn't picked his nose again since the first grade.

And D.J.?

She had the *time of her life*...dancing, joking, and laughing with all her new best friends.

About the Author

Ellie Collins

Ellie Collins wrote this debut novel when she was turning eleven and just beginning sixth grade. She wrote amid a very busy extra-curricular schedule, including a spot on both a gymnastics team and a trampoline and tumbling team, as well as taking weekly piano lessons. She's an avid gamer who loves hanging out with friends. Her love of Greek mythology inspires her writing.

www.facebook.com/AuthorEllieCollins/

Fresh Ink Group

Publishing
Free Memberships
Share & Read Free Stories, Essays, Articles
Free-Story Newsletter
Writing Contests

Books
E-books
Amazon Bookstore

Authors
Editors
Artists
Professionals
Publishing Services
Publisher Resources

Members' Websites
Members' Blogs
Social Media

Twitter: @FreshInkGroup
Google+: Fresh Ink Group
Facebook.com/FreshInkGroup
LinkedIn: Fresh Ink Group
About.me/FreshInkGroup
FreshInkGroup.com

Fresh Ink Group

CPSIA information can be obtained
at www.ICGtesting.com
Printed in the USA
FFOW02n0952270318
46015924-46912FF